THE THREE KINGDOMS

RUSSIAN FOLK TALES From Alexander Afanasiev's Collection

Illustrated
by Alexander Kurkin

Raduga Publishers
Moscow

Contents

ISBN 5-05-004390-5

The Animals in the Pit

There was once an old couple whose only possession was a hog. One day the hog went off to the forest to eat acorns. On the way he met a wolf. "Take me with you." "I would," said the hog, "but there's a deep, wide pit on the way, and you won't be able to jump over it." "Oh, yes, I will," said the wolf. So off they set. On they went through the forest until they came to the pit. "Go on, jump," said the wolf. The hog jumped right over to the other side. Then the wolf jumped and fell straight in. The hog ate his fill of acorns and went home. The next day the hog went off to the forest again. On the way he met a bear. "Hog, hog, where are you going?" "To the forest to eat acorns." "Take me with you," said the bear. "I would, but there's a deep, wide pit on the way, and you won't be able to jump over it." I'll jump over it alright," said the bear. They came to the pit. The hog jumped right over to the other side. But the bear jumped and fell straight in. The hog ate his fill of acorns and went home.

The third day the hog went off to the forest again to eat acorns. On the way he met Squint-Eye the Hare. "Good-day to you, hog!" "Good-day, Squint-Eye!" "Where are you going?" "To the forest to eat acorns." "Take me with you." "No, Squint-Eye, there's a deep, wide pit on the way, and you won't be able to jump over it." "What a thing to say! Of course I will!" Off they went and came to the pit. The hog jumped right over to the other side. The hare jumped and landed in the pit. Then the hog ate his fill of acorns and went home.

The fourth day the hog went off to the forest to eat acorns. On the way he met a fox, who also asked the hog to take her with him. "No," said the hog, "there's a deep, wide pit on the way, and you won't be able to jump over it." "Oh, yes, I will," said the fox. And she landed in the pit as well. So now there were four of them down there, and they began racking their brains about how to get food.

"Let's howl without taking a breath for as long as we can and eat the one who stops first," said the fox. So they began to howl. The hare was the first to stop, and the fox went on the longest. So they seized the hare, tore him to pieces and ate him. They grew hungry again and agreed to howl as long as they could and eat the one that stopped first. "If I stop first, you must eat me," said the fox. So they began to howl. This time the wolf was the first to give up, he just couldn't go on any longer. So the fox and the bear seized him, tore him to pieces and ate him.

But the fox cheated the bear. She gave him only a little of the meat and hid the rest to eat when he wasn't looking. The bear grew hungry again and said: "Where do you get food, Mistress Fox?" "Don't you know, Master Bruin? Stick your paw in your ribs, grab hold of them and yank, then you'll find out." The bear did as he was told, yanked at his ribs, and that was the end of him. Now the fox was all alone. After feasting off the bear, she began to feel hungry again.

Now there was a tree by the pit, and in that tree a thrush was building a nest. The fox sat in the pit watching the thrush and said to it: "Thrush, thrush, what are you doung?" "Building a nest." "What for?" "For my children." "Get me some food, thrush. If you don't, I'll gobble your children up." The thrush racked its brains about how to get the fox some food. It flew to the village and brought back a chicken. The fox gobbled up the chicken and said again: "Thrush, thrush, you got me some food, didn't you?" "Yes, I did." "Well, now get me some drink." The thrush racked its brains about how to get the fox some drink. It flew to the village and brought back some food. "And you got me some drink, didn't you?" "Yes, I did." "Well, now get me out of the pit."

The thrush racked its brains about how to get the fox out. Then it dropped sticks into the pit, so many that the fox was able to climb over them out of the pit, lay down by the tree and stretched out. "Now," she said, "you got me some food, didn't you, thrush?" "Yes, I did." "And you got me some drink, didn't you?" "Yes, I did." "And you got me out of the pit, didn't you?" "Yes, I did." "Well, now make me laugh." The thrush racked its brains about how to make the fox laugh. "I'll fly away," it said, "and you follow me." So the thrush flew off to the village and perched on the gate of a rich man's house, while the fox lay down by ghe gate. Then the thrush began to call out: "Mistress, mistress, give me a

knob of lard! Mistress, mistress, give me a knob of lard!" Out raced the dogs and tore the fox to pieces.

Oh, I was there and drank mead-wine, it wetted my lips, but not my tongue. They gave me to wear a cloak so gay, but the crows cawed loudly on their way: "Cloak so gay! Cloak so gay!" "Throw it away," I thought they said, so I did straightway. They gave me to wear a cap of red, but the crows cawed loudly as they sped: "Cap of red! Cap of red!" "Cap off head," I thought they said, so I pulled it off—and was left with naught.

Translated by Kathleen Cook

The Cat, the Rooster
and the Fox

There was once an old man who had a cat and a rooster.

One day the old man went to the forest to chop wood, the cat soon followed him with his dinner, and the rooster was left all alone.

By and by a fox came running up. She seated herself under the window and sang out:

> "Come, Friend Rooster, comb of gold,
> You who are so brave and bold,
> Look out of the window, please,
> And you'll get some nice, fresh peas!"

The rooster pushed open the window, stuck out his head and looked round to see who was calling him, and the fox seized him and carried him off with her.

> "Save me, Puss, I beg and pray,
> Fox is dragging me away,
> Beyond the dark forests,
> Beyond the white sands,
> Beyond the blue seas,
> To the thrice-ten lands!"

the rooster cried.

7

The cat heard him. He ran after the fox, got the rooster out of her clutches and brought him back home. "Take care, friend Rooster," said the cat, "do not believe what the fox says or look out of the window, for she will eat you up, bones and all!"

On the next day the old man told the rooster to watch over the house and not to look out of the window and went to the forest again to chop wood, and the cat soon followed with his dinner. The fox, who dearly wanted to eat up the rooster, waited for them to go away and then came up to the house and sang out:

> "Come, Friend Rooster, comb of gold,
> You who are so brave and bold,
> Look out of the window, please,
> And you'll get some nice, fresh peas,
> And some grains of wheat, too!"

The rooster walked up and down the house and stayed mum, and the fox sang her little song again and threw a handful of peas in through the window. The rooster ate the peas and said: "You can't fool me, Fox! I know you want to eat me up, bones and all." "Don't be silly, Rooster!" said the fox. "Why should I eat you! All I want is for you to pay me a visit and see what a nice house I have." And she sang out again:

> "Come, Friend Rooster, comb of gold,
> You who are so brave and bold,
> Look out of the window, please,
> And you'll get some nice, fresh peas,
> And some grains of wheat, too!"

The rooster glanced out of the window and lo! — he found himself in the fox's claws!

> "Save me, Puss, I beg and pray,
> Fox is dragging me away,
> Beyond the thick forests,
> Beyond the dark groves,
> Beyond the steep hills
> Where the wild wind roves...
> She wants to eat me up, bones and all!"

he called.

The cat heard him. He ran after the fox, got the rooster out of her clutches and brought him back home. "Didn't I tell you not to look out of the window if you did not want the fox to seize you and eat you up!" said he. "Take care now, for tomorrow we will be going deeper into the forest."

On the next day the old man was in the forest chopping wood and the cat had just left the house with his dinner when the fox crept up to the window. She sang her song three times over, but, seeing that the rooster made no reply, said:

"What's the matter with you, Rooster, have you turned deaf and dumb?" "You won't fool me, Fox, I won't look out of the window!" the rooster told her. The fox threw a handful of peas and some wheat grains in through the window and sang out again:

> "Come, Friend Rooster, comb of gold,
> You who are so brave and bold,
> Look out of the window, do,
> And my house I'll show to you
> Where I keep some nice, ripe wheat
> Which is very good to eat!"

And she added:

"You can't imagine what treasures I have in my house, Rooster! Come, now, show yourself and forget what the cat told you. Had I wanted to eat you op, I would have done so long ago. I like you, Rooster, I like you very much and I want to teach you the ways of the world. Look out of the window, and I'll go round the corner if you don't want me near." And she squeezed herself against the wall.

The rooster jumped up on a bench, but, not being able to see the fox and wanting to know where she was, he stuck his head out of the window, and the fox seized him and was off with him in a trice! The rooster called to the cat to save him, but the cat did not hear him, and the fox took him behind a clump of fir trees and ate him up. She left nothing but some feathers, which were carried away by the wind. The old man and the cat came home, but the rooster was gone. They grieved and sorrowed for a time, and then they said: "That is what happens when you don't listen to those who wish you well!"

Translated by Irina Zheleznova

The Wolf and the Goat

There was once a goat who built herself a little house in the woods and gave birth to a family of kids. The mother goat would often go out to seek for food, and the kids would lock the door behind her and never so much as show their noses outside. The mother goat would come back, knock at the door and sing out:

> "My kiddies own, my children dear,
> Open the door, for your mother is here!
> By a stream I walked, on a grass-grown bank,
> Of fresh grass I ate, of cool water drank;
> I bring you milk which is rich and sweet,
> It runs from my udder down to my feet!"

The kids would open the door and let in their mother, the mother goat would feed them and go off to the woods again, and they would lock the door behind her just as they had before.

Now, the wolf heard the mother goat call to her kids, and when she had just gone out, he stole up and howled the same song.

And the kids called back: "We hear you, whoever you are, but that isn't our mother's voice. Mother's voice is thin and sweet and the words she says are different." The wolf went away and hid himself, and after a while the mother goat came back home. She knocked at the door and sang out:

> "My kiddies own, my children dear,
> Open the door, for your mother is here!
> By a stream I walked, on a grass-grown bank,

11

Of fresh grass I ate, of cool water drank;
I bring you milk which is rich and sweet,
It runs from my udder down to my feet!"

The kids let in their mother and told her about the wolf and about how he had wanted to eat them up. The mother goat fed the kids, and, before leaving for the woods, told them very sternly indeed that if anyone came to the house, asked to be let in in a gruff voice and not used the very same words as she they were not to let him in on any account. She had no sooner left than the wolf came running up. He knocked at the door and sang out in a thin little voice:

"My kiddies own, my children dear,
Open the door, for your mother is here.
By a stream I walked, on a grass-grown bank,
Of fresh grass I ate, of cool water drank;
I bring you milk which is rich and sweet,
It runs from my udder down to my feet!"

The kids opened the door, and the wolf rushed in and gobbled them all up save for one little kid who had crawled into the stove and hidden himself there.

By and by the mother goat came home, but call and shout as she would no one answered her. She gave the door a push, and seeing that it was unlocked, ran inside. The house was empty, but she glanced into the stove, and lo!—found one little kid there. Great was the mother goat's grief when she heard what had happened to her clildren. Down she dropped on the bench and began sobbing loudly, saying over and over again:

"O my children dear, o my kiddies own,
Why did I ever leave you alone?
For the wicked wolf you opened the door,
Never, I fear, will I see you more!"

The wolf heard her, and, coming into the house, said: "Why do you make me out to be such a villain, Mistress Goat? I would never eat your kind! Do not grieve but come for a walk in the woods with me." "No, Mister Wolf, I'm in no mood for a walk." "Please come, please!" the wolf begged.

They went to the woods and soon came to a hole in the ground with a fire burning in it. It had been used by some robbers for cooking gruel in and they had not doused the flames. "Come, Wolf, let us see shich of us can jump over the hole!" said the mother goat. To this the wolf agreed. He leapt across, but tripped and fell into the fire. His belly burst open from the heat, and out the kids hopped, safe and sound, and ran straight to their mother. And they lived happily ever after. The wiser from year to year they grew and never a day of misfortune knew.

Translated by Irina Zheleznova

The Animals' Winter Home

A bull was walking through the forest, when he met a ram. "Where are you going, ram?" asked the bull. "Away from winter to find summer," said the ram. "Come with me!" So off they went together. On the way they met a pig. "Where are you going, pig," said the bull. "Away from winter to find summer," replied the pig. "Come with us!" The three of them set off. On the way they met a goose. "Where are you going, goose?" asked the bull. "Away from winter to find summer," replied the goose. "Well, follow up!" So the goose followed them. On the way they met a rooster. "Where are you going, rooster?" asked the bull. "Away from winter to find summer," replied the rooster. "Follow us." They went on their way and began to talk among themselves: "What shall we do, brothers? The cold season is coming. How shall we keep warm?" And the bull said to them: "let's build a mouse, or we'll freeze to death in the winter." The ram said: "I've got a nice warm coat—just look at the fleece! I'll get through the winter alright." The pig said: "I'm not afraid of any frosts, I'll bury myself in the ground and get through the winter without a house." The goose said: "And I'll perch in a fir tree, lie on one wing and cover myself with the other. The cold won't hurt me. I'll get through the winter easily." "So will I!" said the rooster. The bull saw it was no good, he'd have to do it on his own. "Do as you like," he said, "but I'm going to build a house." So he built himself a house and went to live in it.

A cold frosty winter came and chilled the animals to the marrow. There was nothing for it, so the ram went to the bull and said: "Let me in to get warm,

brother." "No, ram, you've got a nice warm coat. You'll get through the winter alright. Go away." "If you don't let me in, I'll butt your house and knock out a log, then you'll be cold." The bull thought for a while: "I'd better let him in or I'll freeze to death too," and he let the ram in. Then the pig got cold and came to the bull: "Let me in to get warm, brother." "No, I won't. You can bury yourself in the ground and get through the winter like that!" "If you don't let me in, I'll dig round the posts with my snout and bring your house down." There was nothing for it, so the bull let the pig in. Then up came the goose and the rooster: "Let us in to get warm, brother." "No, I won't. You've each got two wings, you can lie on one and cover yourself with the other. You'll get through the winter easily." "If you don't let me in," said the goose, "I'll peck all the moss from the chinks in your walls, then you'll be cold." "So you won't let me in, eh?" said the rooster. "Then I'll fly up and scrape all the straw off the roof. That'll make you cold." There was nothing for it, so the bull let the goose and the rooster in too.

So they all lived together in the house. The rooster warmed up and began singing songs. A fox heard the rooster singing and longed to gobble up this tasty morsel, but how was she to catch him? She hatched a cunning plan, went to the bear and the wolf and said: "I have found some fine fare for each of us, dear masters: a bull for you, bear, a ram for you, wolf, and a rooster for myself." "Well done, mistress," said the bear and the wolf. "We shall not forget your kind service! Let us go and finish them off, then eat them."

The fox took them to the house. "Open the door, master," she said to the bear. "I will go in first and eat the rooster." The bear opened the door, and the fox ran into the house. The bull saw her and straightway pinned her against the wall with his horns, while the ram butted her sides until she gave up the ghost. "Why is she taking so long over the roosters?" said the wolf. "Open the door, friend Bruin! I'll go in now." "Very well, off you go." The bear opened the door, and the wolf ran into the house. The bull pinned him against the wall with his horns, while the ram butted his sides, and they gave him such a welcome that the wolf soon breathed his last. The bear waited and waited. "Why is he taking so long over the ram? I'd better go in." In he went, and the bull and the ram gave him the same welcome, but he managed to fight his way out and ran away as fast as his legs would carry him.

Translated by Kathleen Cook

The Tale of Ruff Ruffson, Son of Bristle

There once lived fat-bellied Ruff Ruffson, who dwelt in a fine house and was forever telling tales about his fellows! He came upon hard times and drove off to Lake Rostov in a miserable sledge drawn by a three-legged nag. There Ruff Ruffson cried out in a loud voice: "Oh, fish of the lake, both large and small, burbot and sterlet, carp, chub and roach, the last among you all! Let me, Ruff Ruffson, into your lake, I pray. Not for a whole year there to stay, but just to feast for one brief day, eat from your table and listen to your prattle."

So the fish of the lake, both large and small, burbot and sterlet, carp, chub and roach, the last among them all, agreed to let him into the lake for a day. Then Ruff Ruffson went on the rampage, harassing the poor fish everywhere, driving them into the slime and up to the weir.

The fish of the lake grew angry and complained about Ruff Ruffson to Peter Sturgeon the Just: "Oh, Peter Sturgeon the Just! Why does Ruff Ruffson harass us? He asked to come into our lake for a day, then started chasing us all away. Hear and pass judgement, Peter Sturgeon." Peter Sturgeon the Just sent the gudgeon, a little fish, to fetch Ruff Ruffson. The gudgeon hunted for him in the

lake, but could not find him. So Peter Sturgeon the Just sent the pike, a middling fish, to look for him.

With a splash of her tail, the pike dived into the lake and found the ruff under a snag. "Hello, Ruff Ruffson!" "Good-day, Pikey! What brings your here?" "I have come to summon you to Peter Sturgeon, who is to pass judgement; a complaint has been made against you." "By whom?" "By the fish of the lake, both large and small, burbot and sterlet, carp, chub and roach, the last among them all, even she has complained about you, and the catfish too, a simple fellow, with lips so thick he can hardly speak. So let's go to the court, Ruff Ruffson, and see that justice is done." "Oh, no, Pikey, dear! Now just listen here. Come along with me, and we'll go on a spree." The pike refused to go with Ruff Ruffson, and tried to take him to court so that he would get his just deserts. "Sharp as you are of tooth and scale, you won't catch Ruff Ruffson by the tail! Today is Saturday, Pikey. The lasses will gather at my father's house and there will be feasting and carousing. Let's go and have fun, eh, and tomorrow, though it be Sunday, we'll go to the court: at least our bellies will be full."

So the pike agreed and went on a spree with Ruff Ruffson.

He made her drunk, lured her into a barn, locked the door and she was heard of no more.

They waited and waited for Ruff Ruffson to appear in court. At last Peter Sturgeon sent the big catfish to fetch him. With a splash of his tail, the catfish dived into the lake and found the ruff under a snag. "Good-day, son-in-law!" "Hello, father-in-law!" "Come with me to court, Ruff Ruffson. A complaint has been made against you." "By whom?" "By the fish of the lake, both large and small, burbot and sterlet, carp, chub and roach, the last among them all!" Ruff Ruffson was the catfish's son-in-law, so there was nothing left for him but to go. "Why have you called me here, Peter Sturgeon the Just?" asked Ruff Ruffson. "Why have I called you indeed! You asked to be let into Lake Rostov for a day, then began chasing all the fish away.

They were greatly angered by this; so the fish of the lake, both large and small, burbot and sterlet, carp, chub and roach, the last among them all, complained to me about you and asked me to pass judgement on the matter!" "Well, now hear my complaint too," replied Ruff Ruffson. "It is they who have wronged me by splashing about and washing away the banks. I was driving past in a hurry and fell into the lake! Summon the king's fishermen, Peter Sturgeon the Just, cast fine nets and drive the fish into the weir, then you will see who is right and who is wrong. For the one who is right will get out of the plight and leap free out of the net."

Peter Sturgeon heard his request, summoned the king's fishermen and drove all the fish into the weir.

Ruff Ruffson got caught in a net. He began twisting and thrashing, with eyes a-popping, and was the first to leap free. "Now do you see who was right and who was wrong, Peter Sturgeon the Just?" "I see that you were right, Ruff Ruffson; go back to the lake and swim at your ease. No one will vex you now, unless the lake dries up and the crows drag you out of the mud." So Ruff Ruffson went down into the lake, boasting for all to hear: "Now fish of the lake, both large and small, burbot and sterlet, carp and chub, you're all in trouble. Nor shall I forgive the roach, the last of them all. Or the fat-bellied catfish. Too thick-lipped to speak, but he knows how to complain! I'll get even with the lot of you!"

Up came Akim and didn't like this bragging; up came Innokenty with stakes a-plenty; up came Maxim and drove the stakes in; up came Gleb and spread out a net; up came Demian and caught the ruffian; then up came Ustin and Ruff slipped free.

Translated by Kathleen Cook

The Fox and the Crane

A fox and a crane became friends. The fox wanted to give her friend the crane a treat and invited him to dinner.

"Come and have dinner with me, Brother Crane, I'll give you an excellent meal!"

The crane accepted the invitation and the fox made some porridge and spread it on plates.

"Eat it all up, Brother Crane," said the fox, "it's very good, I made it myself."

The crane pecked and pecked at the plate with his long beak; he pecked and pecked but could not get anything off the plate.

Meanwhile the fox was licking her plate with her tongue; she licked and licked until the plate was quite clean. She ate up all the porridge herself.

"Don't be angry with me, Brother Crane, but that's all I have in the house. There's nothing else to eat."

"Thank you for that, Sister Fox," answered the crane. "Now you must come and have dinner with me one day."

The fox went to the crane for dinner. The crane had made some soup and put it in tall jars with narrow necks. He put the jars on the table and said:

"Eat it all up, Sister Fox. It's all I have in the house."

The fox walked round and round her jar. She tried this way and that, she licked it, she sniffed it, but not a drop of that soup could she get, for her head was too big to go into the neck of the jar.

But the crane had his long beak in the jar and pecked and pecked until he had eaten all the soup.

"Don't be angry with me, Sister Fox, but that's really all I have in the house."

But the fox *was* angry. She had thought she would eat enough to last her a week, but she went home hungry, as hungry as she had come. The crane had given her tit for tat.

Since then there has been no friendship between the fox and the crane.

Translated by Bernard Isaacs

The Greedy Old Woman

There once lived an old man and an old woman. One day the old man went to the forest to chop wood. He found an old tree and was about to set to work, but the tree said in a human voice: "Spare me, Old Man, and I will do for you whatever you wish." "All right, then, make me rich." "Very well! Go home, and you'll find that you'll have everything you want waiting for you." The old man came home, and lo!—in place of the old hut stood a new one, and it was full of everything! There was money enough to burn, flour enough to last him and his old woman for dozens of years, and there were so many cows, horses and sheep in the barnyard that it would have taken three days and over to count them all. "Where did all this come from, Old Man?" "I found a tree that says it will give me whatever I ask for."

A month passed, and the old woman said "What good does it to us when people show up no respect! "If the steward wants to, he can make us work very hard, and if there's something he doesn't like, he can have us flogged. Go back to the tree and ask it to make you a steward." The old man went to the forest and up to the tree and made as if to chop it down. "What do you want, Old Man?" the tree asked. "I want to become a steward." "Very well. And now go with God!"

He came back home, and lo!—he had been made a steward, and there were soldiers waiting for him who wanted him to find them quarters in the village.

"Where have you been, you old devil?" they shouted. "Find us quarters, quick!" Seeing that a steward too does not always get the respect due him, the old woman said: "What's the good of being a steward! The soldiers gave you a

24

beating, so what is there to say about the landlord: he'll do whatever he wants with you. Go to the forest and ask the tree to make you a landlord."

The old man took his axe, went to the forest and up to the tree and made as if to chop it down. "What do you want, Old Man?" the tree asked. "I want to become a landlord." "Very well. And now go with God!"

The old man became a landlord, but after leading a life of leisure for some time the old woman felt it was not enough and said to the old man: "What's the good of you being a landlord! Now, were you a colonel it would be a different matter, for everyone would envy us." And she told the old man to go and ask the tree to make him a colonel. The old man took his axe, went to the forest and up to the tree and made as if to chop it down. "What do you want, Old Man?" the tree asked. "I want to become a colonel," the old man said. "Very well, a colonel you shall be! And now go with God!" The old man came back home, and lo!—he had been made colonel.

Some time passed, and the old woman said. "Being a colonel isn't all that much. You could be put in the guardhouse by a general if he so wished. Go to the tree, Old Man, and say that you want to become a general." The old man went to the forest and up to the tree and made as if to chop it down with his axe. "What do you want, Old Man?" the tree asked. "I want to become a general." "Very well. And now go with God!" The old man came back home, and lo!—he had been made general.

Some more time passed, and the old woman, who was no longer content being a general's wife, said to the old man:

"Being a general isn't all that much! If the king so wishes, he can exile you to Siberia. Go to the tree and ask it to make you a king and me a queen." Off went the old man to the forest and up to the tree and made as if to chop it down with his axe. "What is it you want, Old Man?" the tree asked. "I want to be king." "Very well. Go with God!" The old man came back home, and there were envoys there waiting to take him to the palace. "The king is dead," said they, "and you have been made king in his stead."

The old man and old woman had not reigned very long when the old woman decided that it wasn't enough to be a queen. So she called the old man and said: "To be king isn't all that much! If God so wills, he'll send death after you and you'll find yourself dead and buried. Go to the tree and ask it to make gods of us." Off went the old man to see the tree, but when it had heard out his mad speeches, it rustled its leaves and said: "Not gods shall you be, both of you, but bears!" And the same moment the old man turned into a he-bear and the old woman into a she-bear, and away they ran into the deep of the forest.

Translated by Irina Zheleznova

Baba-Yaga and Puny

There once lived a man and his wife who had no children. They did all they could, they prayed to God to help them, but God did not seem to hear them. One day the man went to the forest to gather mushrooms and he met an old man on the way. "I know what's on your mind," the old man said. "You want a child. Well, then, what you must do is go from house to house in your village, ask each of your neighbours for an egg and then put a brood-hen on them. You'll see what comes of it!" The man went back to the village, and as there were forty-one houses there and he made the rounds of them all, he collected forty-one eggs, and, this done, put a brood-hen on them. Two weeks passed, and the couple were amazed to see that forty-one babies, all boys, were hatched out of the eggs. Forty of the boys were strong and healthy, but the forty-first was frail and puny. The man began giving the boys names, but could think of only forty and was at a loss to think of a forty-first. "Well," said he to the forty-first boy, "you're frail and puny, so Puny you shall be!"

The boys grew fast, not by the day but by the hour, and when they had grown to manhood, began to help their mother and father, the first forty working in the field and Puny doing the things that needed to be done in the house. Mowing time came, and the forty brothers cut the grass and made hayricks, and after they had worked for a week, came back home. They had their supper and went to bed, and the father looked at them and said: "Look at those lads! They eat a lot, they sleep soundly, but I don't suppose they've done much work!" "Go

27

to the field and see for yourself before you say that, Father," Puny said. The father harnessed a horse and drove to the meadow, and what was his surprise when he saw forty hayricks there! "Good lads to have cut so much grass and put up so many hayricks in one week!" he cried.

On the following day the father again set out for the meadow, for he wanted to feast his eyes on the hayricks. But when he came there he saw that one of the hayricks was gone! He came back home and told his sons about it. "Never mind, Father, we'll find the thief," Puny said. "Give me a hundred rubles and I'll do it myself." The father gave him a hundred rubles, and he went to a smithy and asked the smith if he could forge a chain long enough to bind a man with from head to toe. "And why not!" said the smith. "Well, then, make it as strong as you can. If I find that it's as strong as I want it to be, you'll get a hundred rubles, but if it breaks, then all your labours will have been in vain." The smith forged an iron chain, but when Puny wound it round himself and then pulled at it, it up and broke! The smith then forged him another chain, twice as thick, and finding it to be good and strong, Puny took it, paid the smith his hundred rubles and made for the meadow. He sat down under a hayrick and waited to see what would happen.

Midnight came, the wind began to blow, the sea rose in waves, and from out of its depths stepped a mare. She ran up to the first hayrick and began eating the hay. And Puny jumped up, threw his chain round the mare and sprang on her back. The mare kicked and reared and she carried him over hills and dales, but he sat on her back firmly, and, seeing that she could not throw him, she stopped and said: "Since you were able to get the better of me, my brave lad, you shall have my colts for your own!" She ran to the blue sea and gave a loud whinny, the sea rose in waves, and on to the shore stepped forty-one colts. Each of them was better than the other, and you could not find their like even if you were to search all over the world! Morning came, and the father heard a great pounding of hooves and a loud neighing coming from outside. He rushed out into the yard with his sons, and whom should they see there but Puny leading in a whole herd of horses! "Greetings to you, brothers!" Puny said. "There's a horse here for each of us. Let us go to seek brides for ouselves!" "A good idea!" the brothers said. The mother and father blessed them and off they set on their way.

Long did they ride over the wide world, but where could they find so many brides all in one place! For, not wanting to hurt one another's feelings, they had all of them set their hearts on marrying at one and the same time. On rode the brothers, beyond the thrice-nine lands, and they came to a steep mountain on top of which stood a great house of white stone with a high wall around it and forty-one iron pillars at the gate. They tied their horses to the pillars and went in through the gate into the yard, and whom should they see coming toward them but Baba-Yaga the Witch. "How dared you tie your horses to the pillars without asking, you who come here uninvited!" said she. "Why do you shout, old one? First steam us in the baths and give us food and drink and then ask your

29

question." Baba-Yaga steamed them in the baths and gave them food and drink and then she said: "Come, my brave lads, tell me, have you some purpose in mind or do you come merely to while away the time?" "We have a purpose in mind, Grandma." "And what is it?" "We wish to marry and are seeking brides for ourselves." "I have many daughters," said Baba-Yaga, and she hurried into the house and was soon back, bringing forty-one maids with her.

Each of the brothers then chose himself a bride, a great wedding feast was held, and they all drank and made merry. Evening came, and Puny went to see how his mare was faring. The mare saw him and said in a human voice: "Mind this, master! Before going to bed you must put on your brides' clothes and have them put on yours! If you do not do this, it'll be the end for all of us." Puny passed on to his brothers what the mare had said, and they put on their brides' clothes and had them put on theirs and went to bed. They were soon asleep, all save Puny who never closed an eye. Midnight struck, and Baba-Yaga called out in a loud voice: "Make haste, my faithful servants, cut off the heads of these guests of ours!" And the servants came running and cut off the heads of Baba-Yaga's forty-one daughters. Puny then woke his brothers and told them what had happened and they took the heads and stuck them on the iron poles that surrounded the wall. Then they saddled their horses and made off in great haste.

Morning came, Baba-Yaga rose and looked out of the window, and there, crowning the poles, were her daughters' heads! She flew into a passion, and, ordering her fiery shield to be brought, rode off in pursuit. Where were the brothers to hide? Ahead of them lay the blue sea, and behind them came Baba-Yaga burning everything in her way with her shield! Death seemed close, but Puny was a clever lad and had not forgotten to take along Baba-Yaga's magic kerchief. He waved the kerchief in front of him, a bridge spanning the blue sea rose before him, and he and his brothers crossed it and were soon on the opposite shore. Then Puny waved the kerchief behind him, the bridge vanished, Baba-Yaga was forced to turn back, and the brothers rode safely home.

Translated by Irina Zheleznova

The Swan-Geese

There once lived a man and a woman who had a little daughter and a son who was still a baby. One day the mother and father prepared to go to the field, and the mother said to the daughter: "Your father and I are going out to work, child, and if you will be a good and a clever girl, take good care of your little brother and never leave the yard, we will bring you back a bun, buy you a kerchef and make you a pretty dress." The mother and father went away, and the little girl never gave her mother's words a thought. She seated her brother on the grass under the window and herself ran out into the street where she began playing with friends and got so caught up in the games that she quite forgot what she had been told. All of a sudden a flock of Swan-Geese came flying up. They swept up the little boy and carried him off on their wings.

The girl came home, and her brother was not there! She oh'd and ah'd and rushed about looking for him, but there was not a sign of him anywhere! She called to him, and she wept and sobbed, saying over and over again that her mother and father would punish her, but he never replied. Now, the Swan-Geese were known to be wicked birds who did much evil and stole little children, and so, guessing that it was they who had carried off her brother, she decided to run after them and to try and overtake them. She ran and she ran and she came to an oven. "Please, Oven, tell me where the Swan-Geese have flown," said she. "Eat one of my rye buns, and I will." "A rye bun? Never! Why, at home we don't even eat wheaten buns!" The oven kept mum and would tell her nothing, and the girl ran on. By and by she came upon an apple-tree. "Please, Apple-Tree, tell me

31

where the Swan-Geese have flown," said she. "Eat one of my wild apples, and I will!" "Not I! Why, at home we don't even eat garden apples!" On she ran, and she came to a river of milk with fruit jelly banks. "Please, milk river with fruit jelly banks, tell me where the Swan-Geese have flown," said she. "Eat some of my jelly with milk and I will." "Not I! Why, at home we don't even eat jelly with cream!"

The girl ran on, and she would have been roaming the fields and woods to this day if she hadn't been lucky enough to meet a hedgehog. She wanted to push it away, but did not, for she was afraid of getting pricked. "Please, Hedgehog, tell me, have you seen where the Swan-Geese have flown?" she asked. "Over there!" And he showed her where. On she ran and she came to a hut on chicken feet which kept runing round and round. Inside the hut sat Baba-Yaga the Witch with a face lined and grey and a leg of clay, and on a bench beside her sat the little girl's brother playing with some golden apples. The girl crept up to him, seized him and carried him off with her. But the Swan-Geese, wicked birds that they were, flew after her and if she did not want to get into their clutches she had to find some place to hide. There before her was the milk river with the fruit jelly banks, and she bent over it and said: "Please, River, be a mother to me and hide me." "Have some of my fruit jelly first!" There was nothing to be done, so she had some of the jelly. The river hid her under its bank, and the Swan-Geese flew past and never saw her. She thanked the river and ran on with her brother, but the Swan-Geese had turned back and were flying straight toward her. What was the girl to do! There before her was the apple-tree, so she turned to it and said: "Please, Apple-Tree, be a mother to me and hide me!" "Eat one of my wild apples, and I will!" The girl ate one quickly, and the apple-tree hid her and her little brother among its leaves and branches. The Swan-Geese flew past, and the little girl picked up her brother and ran on. The Swan-Geese saw her and flew after her. They were very close now, they flapped their wings and were about to tear her brother out of her arms at any moment! Luckily, there was the oven just in front of her. "Please, Mistress Oven, hide me!" she begged. "Have one of my rye buns, and I will!" The girl popped a ruy bun into her mouth and herself crawled into the oven, The Swan-Geese flew round and round, screaming and honking, but after a while gave up and flew away. The little girl ran home with her brother, and she got there just in time, for her mother and father came in right after her.

Translated by Irina Zheleznova

Right and Wrong

In a certain realm there lived two peasants, Ivan and Naum. They made friends and set off together to look for work. On and on they went until they came to a prosperous village and hired themselves out to different masters. They worked for a week and met up on Sunday. "How much have you earned, brother?" asked Ivan. "The Lord has given me five rubles." "The Lord! He won't give you a brass farthing, if you don't earn it for yourself." "No, you are wrong, brother. Without the Lord's help you can do nothing, not even earn a farthing!" Theroupon they began to argue and at last agreed on this: "We'll both walk along the road and ask the first person we meet who is right. The one who loses must give all the money he has earned to the other." So off they went. They had barely gone twenty paces, when they met an evel spirit in human guise. They asked him their question, and he replied: "What you earn, you earn yourself. It's no good relying on the Lord. He won't give you a brass frathing!" So Naum gave all his money to Ivan and returned to his master empty-handed. Another week passed. The following Sunday the two men met again and had the same argument. Naum said: "Even though you took all my money last week, the Lord has given me more!" "Well," said Ivan, "if you really think that the Lord gave it to you and not that you earned it, let's ask the first person we meet again who is right. The one who is wrong must hand over all his moeny and lose his right arm." Naum consented.

Off they went along the road and met the evel spirit again, who gave the same answer as before. Ivan took his friend's money, cut off his right arm and left

him there. Naum wondered what he would do now without an arm and who would feed him. But the Lord is merciful! He went to the river and lay down on the bank under a boat. "I'll spend the night here and dicide what to do in the morning. Morning's wiser than evening."

At the stroke of midnight a host of evil spirits assembled in the boat and began to boast of the mischief they had wrought. One said: "I gave false judgement in a quarrel between two men, and the man who was right had his arm cut off." To which another replied: "That's nothing! He need only roll in the dew three times and his arm will grow again!" "I put the evel eye on a rich man's only daughter and she's almost wasted away!" bragged a third. "Listen to that!" sneered a fourth. "Anyone who feels sorry for the man can easily cure his daughter. Just get hold of such-and-such a plant, boil it up and bathe her in the water. She'll be as fit as a fiddle!" "I know a man who built a water mill and has worked hard for years, all for nothing. As soon as he finishes the weir, I make a hole in it and let the water out..." "Your miller's a fool!" scoffed a sixth evil spirit. "He should line the weir with brushwood and throw a sheaf of hay in when the water begins to run out: that would be the end of you!"

Naum overheard all this. The next day he made his right arm grow again, fixed the miller's weir and cured the rich man's daugher. The miller and the rich man rewarded him generously, and he began to prosper. One day he met his old friend, who was most surprised and asked him how he had made his money and got his right arm back. Naum told him the whole story, concealing nothing. Ivan listened and thought: "Why don't I do the same and get even richer!" He went to the river and lay down on the bank under the boat. At midnight the evil spirits assembled. "Someone must be eavesdropping, brothers," said one of them. "That man's arm has grown again, the rich man's daughter is cured, and the weir is working properly."

They rushed to look under the boat, found Ivan and made mincemeat of him. And so the biter was bit!

Translated by Kathleen Cook

Prince Ivan
and Princess Martha

A certain king had a copper man with arms of steel and a head of iron, a very artful character, whom he kept locked up in prison. The king's son, Prince Ivan, was still a little boy. One day as he walked past the prison, the old man called him over and said to him: "Please give me a drink, Prince Ivan!" Prince Ivan was too small to know better, so he got some water and gave it to him, whereupon the old man slipped out of the prison and vanished. Word of this reached the king, who ordered Prince Ivan to be banished from the realm. The king's word is law. So Prince Ivan was banished forthwith and set off on his wanderings.

On and on he went until he came to another kingdom, went straight to the king and asked him for work. The king took him in and made him a stable-boy. He did nothing but doze all day in the stables and would not look after the horses. The head groom often beat him. But Prince Ivan bore it all patiently. Then another king asked for this king's daughter in marriage and was refused, so he declared war. Our king went off with his army, liaving his fair daughter Princess Martha to rule the land. She had noticed that the stable-boy was not of common stock and sent him off to be the governor of somewhere or other.

Prince Ivan went to live and rule there. One day he decided to go hunting. He had just set off when the copper man with arms of steel and a head of iron popped up out of thin air. "Good-day, Prince Ivan!" Prince Ivan returned his

37

greeting. "Come and be my guest," said the man. So off they went. The old man took him to a rich house and called to his youngest daughter: "Bring us food and drink, and a gallon-sized goblet of liquor!" They began to dine. The daughter brought in the gallon-sized goblet of liquor and took it up to Prince Ivan. He refused it saying: "I couldn't manage all that!" The old man told him to have a try. So he picked up the goblet and suddenly found the strength to drain it in a single draught.

Then the old man took him out to try his strength. They came to a stone weighing five hundred poods. "Pick up this stone, Prince Ivan," the old man said. "I can't lift that," Prince Ivan thought to himself. "But I'll have a go." He picked it up and tossed it like a feather. "Where did I get the strength?" he wondered again. "It must have been in that liquor the old man gave me." They strolled on for a while, then turned back. When they came back to the house, the old man called to the middle daughter to bring two gallons of liquor. Prince Ivan grasped the goblet boldly and drained it in a single draught. They went out for a walk again and came to a stone weighing a thousand poods. "Now toss this stone!" said the old man. Prince Ivan pcked up the stone and tossed it like a feather. "What strength I have inside me!" he thought to himself.

Then back they went, and the old man called to the eldest daughter to bring a three-gallon goblet of liquor. Prince Ivan drained this too in a single draught. He and the old man went out for a walk. Prince Ivan tossed a stone weighing two thousand poods with the greatest of ease. Then the old man gave him a magic table-cloth and said: "There is great strength inside you now, Prince Ivan. Your horse cannot carry you! Strengthen the porch of your house, for it will not bear your weight either. Get new chairs. And put more supports under the floors. God be with you!" People laughed to see the governor returning from the hunt on foot, leading his horse by the bridle. When he got home, he ordered them to put more supports under the floors and make new chairs. He sent away the cooks and chambermaids and lived on his own like a hermit. Nobody cooked for him, and people marvelled that he did not need to eat. The magic table-cloth was feeding him all the time, of course.

He never went visiting, and indeed how could he? The houses could not bear his weight.

Meanwhile the king returned from the wars, heard that Prince Ivan was a governor and had him replaced and sent back to the stables. There was nothing for it, so Prince Ivan became a stable-boy again. One day the head groom gave him some orders and hit him. Prince Ivan lost his temper, seized the head groom and knocked his head off. Word of this reached the king. He summoned Prince Ivan. "Why did you strike the groom?" asked the king. "He hit me first, Your Majesty, so I hit him back, not very hard, on the head. And his head just fell off." The other stable-boys said the same thing. The head groom had hit Prince Ivan first, and Prince Ivan hit him back; but not very hard. The king did nothing

to Prince Ivan, only made him a soldier indstead of a stable-boy. So Prince Ivan went off to the army.

Not long after this a thumb-sized mannikin with a long, long beard brought a letter bearing three black seals from the Water King. It said that if the king did not deliver his daughter, Princess Martha, to such-and-such an island on such-and-such a day to marry the Water King's son, he would kill the lot of them and burn the whole kingdom to ashes. A three-headed dragon would collect Princess Martha. The king read the letter and sent a reply to the Water King consenting to the match. He saw the mannikin off and summoned together his senators and ministers to think up a way of saving his daughter from the three-headed dragon. If he did not deliver her to the island, the whole kingdom would be destroyed by the Water King. A proclamation was issued calling for someone to save Princess Martha from the dragon. The king promised his daugher's hand in return for this service.

A fine gentleman volunteered. He took a regiment of soldiers and set off with Princess Martha for the island. There he left her in a cabin and waited outside for the dragon. Meanwhile Prince Ivan heard that Princess Martha had been taken to the Water King and he set off for the island too. He came to the cabin, where Princess Martha was weeping. "Do not weep, Princess," he said to her. "God is merciful!" He lay down on the bench with his head on Princess Martha's lap and fell fast asleep. Suddenly the dragon began to rise out of the water, sending up a wave ten feet high. The fine gentleman was with the soldiers. When the water began to rise, he ordered: "Quick march, into the forest." Off scurried the soldiers into the forest. The dragon came out and made straight for the cabin. Princess Martha saw it coming for her and woke Prince Ivan. He jumped up, cut off the dragon's three heads with one fell swoop, and went away. The fine gentleman took Princess Martha home to her father.

Not long after that the thumb-sized mannikin with the long, long beard came out of the water again bearing a letter with six black seals from the Water King asking the king to deliver his daughter to a six-headed dragon on the self-same island. If he did not, the Water King threatened to flood the whole kingdom. The king once more wrote consenting to deliver Princess Martha. The mannikin went away. The king issued a proclamation, and notices were put up all over the land, calling for someone to save Princess Martha from the dragon. The same fine gentleman turned up and said: "I'll save her, Your Majesty, only give me a regiment of soldiers." "Don't you need more than that? It's a six-headed dragon this time." "That will do. It's more than enough for me."

They made ready and went off with Princess Martha. Prince Ivan learnt that Princess Martha was in danger again and, remembering her kindness in making him a governor, he set off once again, on foot or horseback, I cannot say. He found Princess Martha in the cabin and went in to her. She was waiting for him and was overjoyed to see him. He lay down and fell fast asleep. Suddenly the six-headed dragon began to rise out of the water, sending up a wave twenty feet high. The fine gentleman and the soldiers were safe in the forest. The dragon made for the cabin. Princess Martha woke Prince Ivan. He and the dragon grappled and fought. Prince Ivan cut off one head, another, a third, then all the rest, threw them into the water and walked away as cool as a cucumber. The fine gentleman came out of the forest with the soldiers, went back and told the king that the lord had helped him to save Princess Martha. He must have threatened her in some way, for she dared not say that someone else had rescued her. The fine gentleman wanted them to fix the wedding day there and then. But Princess Martha said they must wait. "Give me time to get over the shock," she said. "I had a really nasty fright."

Suddenly the thumb-sized mannikin with the long, long beard came out of the water again bearing a letter with nine black seals that asked the king to deliver Princess Martha to a nine-headed dragon on such-and-such an island and such-and-such a day and said that if he did not his whole kingdom would be flooded. The king again wrote his consent, then set about looking for someone to save the princess from the nine-headed dragon. The same fine gentleman volunteered again and set off with a regiment of soldiers and Princess Martha.

Prince Ivan heard of this, made ready and set off to where Princess Martha was waiting for him. When he arrived, she was overjoyed and asked him who he was, what he was called and who his parents were. He said nothing, but lay down and fell fast asleep. Then the nine-headed dragon began to rise out of the water, sending up a wave thirty feet high. "Quick march into the forest!" the fine gentleman ordered the soldiers. Off they scurried. Princess Martha tried to wake Prince Ivan, but in vain. The dragon was on the threshold. She burst into tears; for she could not rouse Prince Ivan. The dragon slithered up to Prince Ivan! He lay fast asleep. Now Princess Martha had a penknife. She gashed Prince Ivan's cheek with it. He awoke, sprang to his feet, and grappled with the dragon. The dragon began to get the better of Prince Ivan. Suddenly out of thin air up popped the copper man with arms of steel and a head of iron. Together they chopped off all the dragon's heads, threw them into the water and went away. The fine gentleman was as pleased as punch; he hopped out of the forest, went back to his kingdom and began pestering the king to fix the wedding day there and then. Princess Martha kept saying: "Wait till I've got over the shock. That was a really nasty fright."

The thumb-sized mannikin with the long, long beard brought another letter. The Water King demanded to have the guilty person. The fine gentleman didn't want to go to the Water King, but they made him. A boat was prepared and off they set. Prince Ivan happened to be serving in the navy and somehow managed to be on the same boat. Suddenly they met another boat, flying like the wind. "Who is the guilty one? Who is the guilty one?" came the shouts from it as it sped past. A little later they met another boat. "Who is the guilty one? Who is the guilty one?" Prince Ivan pointed to the fine gentleman. They beat him to within an inch of his life and sailed on.

Then they came to the Water King. The Water King ordered an iron bath to be filled to the top with boiling water and the guilty person to be put into it. The fine gentleman took fright. His heart sank into his boots! This was the end! But with Prince Ivan was a man from the navy who had seen that Prince Ivan was not of common stock and stayed to serve him. Prince Ivan said to him: "Go and sit in the bath." The servant ran off and did as he was told, and nothing happened to the devil. He came back unscathed. Again the guilty one was summoned, this time to appear before the Water King himself. They took the fine gentleman to him. The Water King cursed him roundly, beat him soundly, and bade them take him away. So back home they all went.

At home the fine gentleman was more conceited than ever and kept pestering the king to name the wedding day. The king agreed and the date was fixed. You should have seen how high and mighty the fine gentleman got then, strutting around and looking down his nose at everybody. But the princess said to her father: "Have all the soldiers lined up, Sire. I want to inspect them." No sooner said than done. Princess Martha walked up and down until she came to Prince Ivan. She looked at his cheek and saw the scar from the cut with the penknife. Then she took Prince Ivan by the hand and led him to her father. "Here is the man who rescued me from the dragon, Sire. I didn't know who he was, but now I recognise him by the scar on his cheek. The fine gentleman hid in the forest with the soldiers!" Straightway the soldiers were asked if this were really so. "Yes, Your Majesty," they replied. "The fine gentleman was scared out of his wits!" So the fine gentleman was stripped of all his honours; but Prince Ivan married Princess Martha and they lived happily ever after.

Translated by Kathleen Cook

The Three Kingdoms

In a certain kingdom, in a certain realm there lived a king by the name of
Bel-Belianin who had a wife named Nastasya the Golden Plait and three sons,
Prince Pyotr, Prince Vassily and Prince Ivan. One day the queen and her women
and maids went for a walk in the garden. All of a sudden a great whirlwind arose
and it caught up the queen, which God forbid should happen to anyone, and
carried her off none knew where.

The king was very sad and woebegone and did not know what to do, but
when his sons had grown to manhood he said to them: "My dear sons, my
beloved sons, will not one of you go to seek your mother?" The two elder sons
did not delay but set off at once, and the third and youngest son began pleading
with his father to let him go too. "No, my son, you mustn't leave me, an old
man, all alone," said the king. "Please let me go, Father! I do so want to travel
over the world and find my mother." The king reasoned with him, but, seeing
that he could not stop him from going, said: "Oh, all right then, I suppose it
can't be helped. Go and God be with you!"

Prince Ivan saddled his trusty steed and set forth from home. Whether he was
long on the way or not nobody knows, for a tale is quick in the telling and a deed
is slow in the doing, but by and by he came to a forest where stood a most
beautiful palace. Prince Ivan rode into the yard, and a large yard it was, and,
seeing an old man coming toward him, said: "Good morrow, old man, and many
long years of life to you!" "Welcome, welcome, my brave lad! And who may you

43

be?" "I am Prince Ivan, son of King Bel-Belianin and Queen Nastasya the Golden Plait." "Then you are my own nephew! Whither are you bound?" "I am seeking my mother. Do you know where she is to be found, Uncle?" "No, my lad, I don't. But I'll do what I can for you. Here is a little ball. Throw it down before you, and it will start rolling and bring you to a tall, steep mountain with a cave in it. Go into the cave, take the iron claws that you will see there, fit them on to your hands and feet and climb the mountain. You may well find your mother on its top."

Well and good, Prince Ivan bade his uncle farewell and threw the ball before him. On the ball rolled, and he rode after it. Whether a short or a long time passed nobody knows, but by and by he came to a field and whom should he see there but his brothers Prince Pyotr and Prince Vassily surrounded by a host of fighting men. The brothers rode forth to meet him. "Where are you going, Prince Ivan?" they asked. "I got bored staying at home and thought I would go to seek our mother. Send your men home and come with me." The brothers did as he said. They sent the men home and joined him, and the three of them followed the ball together.

By and by they saw the mountain, and so tall and steep was it that it touched the sky with its peak! The ball rolled up straight to a cave, and Prince Ivan got off his horse and said to his brothers: "Stay here and look after my horse, brothers, and I will climb the mountain and try to find our mother. Wait for me for three months, and if I am not back by then, you will know that it's no use waiting any longer." "A man can break his neck climbing a mountain like that!" thought the brothers, but they said to him: "Very well, then, go with God and we will wait for you here."

Prince Ivan came up to the cave, gave its door of iron a mighty push and sent it flying open. He came inside, and the iron claws jumped up and fixed themselves to his hands and feet. But it took all of his strength to climb the mountain, and a whole month passed before he at last reached its top. "God be thanked, I'm here at last!" said he. He rested awhile and then went on. He walked and he walked, and, standing before him, saw a palace of copper. Chained to the gate with copper chains were the most fearful of dragons, while close by was a well with a copper dipper dangling at the end of a copper chain. Prince Ivan scooped up some water and gave the dragons a drink, and, thus having quietened them, passed on into the palace where he was met by the Princess of the Copper Kingdom.

"Who are you, brave youth?" she asked. "I am Prince Ivan." "Is it of your own free will that you have come here, Prince Ivan, or at another's bidding?" "Of my own free will. I am seeking my mother, Nastasya the Golden Plait, who was carried off by Whirlwind. Do you happen to know where she is?" "No, I don't. But my middle sister the Princess of the Silver Kingdom, lives nearby, and she may know." And she brought out a copper ball and a copper ring and gave them to him. "This ball," said she, "will lead you to my middle sister, and in this ring

is the whole of my Copper Kingdom. When you have vanquished Whirlwind, who keeps me captive here and comes to see me every three months, do not forget me, unhappy soul that I am, but deliver me from captivity and take me with you to where I can be free." "Very well, I'll do that," said Prince Ivan. He cast the copper ball down on the ground, started it rolling and went after it.

He came to the Silver Kingdom and saw before him a palace that was made of silver and was even more beautiful than the copper one. Chained with silver chains to the gate were fearful dragons, and close by was a well with a silver dipper. Prince Ivan scooped up some water and gave it to the dragons to drink, and they lay down on the ground and let him pass on into the palace where he was met by the princess of the Silver Kingdom. "It will be three years soon that I have been kept here by Whirlwind, and I have not seen a Russian face or heard Russian speech in all that time," said she. "Who are you, brave youth?" "I am Prince Ivan." "Have you come here of your own free will or at another's bidding?" "Of my own free will. I am seeking my mother whom Whirlwind seized when she was out walking in the garden and carried off none knows where. Do you know where I can find her?" "No, I don't. But my elder sister, Elena the Fair, the Princess of the Golden Kingdom, lives nearby, and she may know. Here is a silver ball for you. Send it rolling and follow it, and it will lead you to the Golden Kingdom. And when you have killed Whirlwind do not forget me, unhappy soul that I am, but deliver me from captivity and take me with you to where I can be free. For Whirlwind keeps me captive here and comes to see me every two months." She gave him a silver ring and said: "My whole Silver Kingdom is in this ring." And Prince Ivan sent the silver ball rolling along and went after it.

Whether a short or a long time passed nobody knows, but by and by he saw before him a palace of gold that flamed like fire. Fearful dragons, chained to the wall with chains of gold, guarded the gate, and close by was a well with a dipper of gold dangling at the end of a gold chain. Prince Ivan scooped up a dipperful of water and gave the dragons a drink, and they quietened and lay down on the ground so that he was able to pass on into the palace. Elena the Fair met him there and asked him who he was. "I am Prince Ivan." "Have you come here of your own free will or at another's bidding?" "Of my own free will. I am seeking my mother, Nastasya the Golden Plait. Do you know where I can find her?" "That I do. She lives nearby, and Whirlwind comes to see her once a week and me, once a month. Here is a gold ball for you. Send it rolling along and go after it, and it will lead you wherever you wish to go. And take this gold ring, too; in it is the whole of the Golden Kingdom. But mind this, Prince Ivan: when you have vanquished Whirlwind, do not forget me, unhappy soul that I am, but take me with you to where I can be free." "I'll not forget you," said the Prince.

He sent the ball rolling along and and went after it, he walked and he walked, and he came to a palace that flamed like fire so many were the diamonds and other gems studding its walls. By the gate were six-headed dragons that hissed as he came near, but Prince Ivan gave them water to drink and they quietened and let him pass on into the palace. Many were the chambers he passed through, and in the last one, sitting on a high throne, he found his mother. She was garbed in royal garments and had on a gem-studded crown. She glanced up as he came in, and seeing who it was, cried: "Dear God in Heaven, is it you, my beloved son? How did you get here?" He told her all about everything and then said: "I have come for you." "It is a hard task you have set yourself, my son," said she. "For the ruler of this mountain is Whirlwind who is as mighty as he is evil and who holds all the spirits in his way. It was he who carried me off, and it is him you will have to grapple with! Now come down into the cellar with me."

They went down into the cellar, and there were two tubs of water there, one standing near the right wall and the other, near the left one. "Drink some water out of the tub that is near the right wall," said Nastasya the Golden Plait. Prince Ivan did as she told him. "How strong do you feel?" she asked him. "So strong that I know I could turn the whole palace round with one hand if I chose!" "Take another sip from the same tub." Prince Ivan bent down and took another sip. "And how strong do you feel now?" "So strong that I know I could turn the whole world upside down!" "That makes you very strong indeed! And now move the tub that is near the right wall to the left wall, and the one near the left wall to the right one." Prince Ivan did as she told him. "The tub you drank from is filled with strong water, my dear son," his mother said, "and the other, with strengthless water. He who drinks of the first will become very, very strong, and he who drinks of the second, very weak. Now, Whirlwind always drinks out of the first tub, which he keeps near the right wall, and if we are to get the better of him we must trick him."

They climbed the cellar stairs and were soon back in the self-same chamber, and his mother told Prince Ivan that Whirlwind would soon be coming home. "Hide under my mantle that he might not see you," she said. "And as soon as he flies in and begins embracing and kissing me, grab hold of his cudgel and don't let go of it. He will rise high into the air and carry you over mountains and seas, but you must never loosen your hold. He will tire after a while, and, wanting to drink of the strong water, come down into the cellar and rush to the tub we have put near the right wall. He will drink from it, and you must drink from the other one. When you see that he has lost all of his strength, you must seize his sword and smite off his head with one blow. When you have done that, you will hear voices telling you to smite again. Do not heed them but say in reply: 'A true knight never smites but once!'"

No sooner had Prince Ivan hidden himself under his mother's mantle than it grew dark outside, everything around them began to shake and to tremble, and Whirlwind came flying up. He struck the ground, turned into a tall and handsome man and came into the palace, a great cudgel in his hand. "Fee-fofum! I smell Russian flesh. Has anyone been here?" "No, and I don't know what makes you think so," the queen said. Whirlwind threw his arms around her and began kissing her, and Prince Ivan grabbed hold of his cudgel. "I'll soon do away with you!" Whirlwind cried. "That remains to be seen. You might and then again you might not." At this Whirlwind flew out through the window and soared to the sky, and he bore Prince Ivan away with him. They flew over a mountain, and Whirlwind said, "I'll dash you to the ground and kill you!" But he could not make good his threats, for Prince Ivan held on to the cudgel and would not let go of it.

Whirlwind flew all round the world, and at last, feeling weary, he came down to the ground and into the cellar. Not knowing that it was filled with strengthless water, he rushed to the tub that stood near the right wall and began drinking from it, and Prince Ivan let him do it and himself drank from the tub that stood near the left wall and that was filled with strong water. Very soon Whirlwind lost all his strength while Prince Ivan became the strongest man that ever lived. Snatching his sabre from him, he smote off Whirlwind's head, and the moment he had done so he heard voices calling from behind him: "Smite again, smite again or he will come back to life!" "No," said Prince Ivan, "a true knight never smites but once." He made up a fire, burnt Whirlwind's head and his body and cast the ashes into the wind. Nastasya the Golden Plait was overjoyed. "Let us now make merry and eat and drink, my son," said she, "and then make haste and set out for home, for this is a dull place with no one to talk to even." "Who is to serve us, then, if no one lives here?" "That you shall see." And before another word was said the table was covered with a cloth, and all sorts of foods and drinks appeared on it. And as they ate, the sound of music fell on their ears and someone they could not see sang to them. They ate and they drank and had a rest, and Prince Ivan said: "It is time to go, Mother! My two brothers are waiting for us at the foot of the mountain, and I still have to free the three Princesses whom Whirlwind has been keeping captive."

They took everything they needed and set out on their way. They freed the three Princesses and taking away a length of cloth as well as many of the fine and costly things they found in the three palaces, went on and soon came to the place where they could begin their descent from the mountain. Prince Ivan tied his mother to the cloth first and let her down on it, and then he let down Elena the Fair and her two sisters. His two brothers stood below watching and said: "We'll leave Prince Ivan on the mountain top, and we'll take our mother and the three Princesses to our father and tell him that it was we who found and freed them." "I will marry Elena the Fair, and you the Princess of the Silver Kingdom," said Prince Pyotr to Prince Vassily, "and the Princess of the Copper Kingdom will have to be content with a general."

It was now the turn of Prince Ivan to let himself down from the mountain, but his brothers seized the bottom end of the cloth and ripped it off. Prince Ivan was left on the top of the mountain and there was nothing he could do. He burst into tears and went back along the road, but though he walked all over the Copper Kingdlom, the Silver Kingdom and the Golden Kingdom, not a soul did he see. He came to the Diamond Kingdom, but there was no one there either, and he felt so lonely he wanted to die. Then, lying on the window sill in one of the palace chambers, he saw a pipe. "I think I'll play a little tune just to keep boredom away," said he picking it up. He put the pipe to his lips and blew, and as if out of nowhere there appeared before him a lame man and a one-eyed man. "What can we do for you, Prince Ivan?" asked they. "I'm hungry. Bring me something to eat." And lo!—quick as lightning the table was set and the best of foods and drinks appeared on it. Prince Ivan ate and then he said to himself: "And now I wouldn't mind having a rest." He put the pipe to his lips and blew, and the lame man and the one-eyed man appeared. "What can we do for you, Prince Ivan?" they asked. "Make a bed for me." No sooner were the words out of his mouth than the bed was made, and it was the softest he had ever slept on.

He had a good sleep and then blew upon his pipe again. "What can we do for you?" asked the lame man and the one-eyed man. "Does that mean that I can ask for anything and it will be done?" asked Prince Ivan. "Yes, anything at all, Prince Ivan. All you have to do is blow upon the pipe. Just as we were ready to serve Whirlwind before, so are we ready to serve you now. Only you must have the pipe with you always." "Good!" said Prince Ivan, and he added: "I wish to be back in my own realm." And no sooner had he said this than he found himself in his own realm, at a market-place. He walked along, and there, coming toward him, he saw a shoemaker, as jolly a fellow as ever lived. "Where are you going, my man?" asked Prince Ivan. "To sell a pair of boots. I'm a shoemaker." "How would you like me to work for you?" "Can you make shoes?" "Yes, and clothes, too. I can do anything." "Good! Come along, then!"

They came to the shoemaker's house, and the shoemaker said: "Now, then, make me a pair of boots out of this piece of leather, and it's fine leather, believe me you. I want to see what you can do." He showed Prince Ivan into the room he was to live in and left him there. Prince Ivan got out his pipe and blew upon it, and the lame man and the one-eyed man appeared before him. "What can we do for you, Prince Ivan?" they asked. "I want you to make me a pair of boots, to be ready by tomorrow." "It shall be done!" "Here, take this piece of leather." "A poor piece, if ever there was one! It ought to be thrown out." Morning came, Prince Ivan rose, and there on the table stood a beautiful pair of boots! The shoemaker too got up from bed. "Are the boots ready?" he asked. "They are," said Prince Ivan. "Well, then, let me see them!" Prince Ivan brought out the boots, and the shoemaker took one look at them and gasped in wonder. "I have found meself a master shoemaker, a man with magic fingers!" he cried. And he took the boots and made for the market-place with them.

Now, at this same time preparations for three weddings were under way in the palace: Prince Pyotr was marrying Elena the Fair, Prince Vassily, the Princess of the Silver Kingdom, and a general the Princess of the Copper Kingdom. Finery of all sorts was being purchased for the brides and grooms, and Elena the Fair said that she needed a pair of boots. Now, as no boots better than the ones the shoemaker was offering could be found, he was at once brought to the palace.

And Elena the Fair took one look at them and said: "Such boots can only have been made in Whirlwind's palace!" She paid the shoemaker a large sum of money and bade him make her another pair. "They must be ornamented with diamonds and other precious stones," said she. "And I will not have you measuring my feet. Just remember this. If they are not ready by breakfast-time tomorrow, you shall be hanged!"

The shoemaker took the money and the gems with which the boots were to be ornamented and left the palace with hanging head. "Unhappy man that I am! What am I to do?" he said to himself. "How can I have the boots ready by tomorrow?" It's the gallows for me and no mistake! I think I had better have a drink or two with my friends before I die." He stepped into an inn where he found some of his friends, of whom he had many, and, seeing him, they asked why he was so glum. "Ah, my friends, I'm to be hanged tomorrow!" "Hanged? What for?" The shoemaker told them about the boots he had been ordered to make. "It's no use trying to work!" said he. "Let's drink and make merry instead." They drank and made merry, and by the time the day was drawing to a close the shoemaker could hardly stand on his feet he was so drunk. "I think I'll take a keg of wine home and go to bed," said he. "And when they come for me tomorrow, I'll down a half of it. A man can't feel the rope round his neck when he's dead drunk." He came home and said to Prince Ivan: "See what those boots of yours have done, curse you! I'm to be hanged. Wake me when they come for me tomorrow morning."

Night came, Prince Ivan got out his pipe and blew upon it, and the lame man and the one-eyed man appeared. "What can we do for you, Prince Ivan?" they asked. "You are to make me a pair of boots to be ready by morning," said he, and he told them what kind of boots were wanted. "It shall be done!" Prince Ivan went to bed and to sleep, and in the morning, there were the boots standing on the table, the gems on them sparkling and glittering. "Time to get up, Master!" he called to the shoemaker. "Have they come for me, then? Bring the keg of wine and pour me a cupful, let them hang me drunk." "But the boots are ready, Master." "What! Where are they?" He rushed into Prince Ivan's room, and, seeing the boots, said: "When did you and I manage to make them?" "During the night, Master. Don't you remember?" "No, I'm that fuzzy, I don't."

He took the boots, wrapped them up and ran to the palace, and when Elena the Fair saw them she at once knew that it was Whirlwind's two servants who had made them. "How ever did you manage to make these boots?" asked she of the shoemaker. "I can do anything!" "If that is so, then make me a wedding dress sewn with gold and studded with diamonds and other precious stones. And it must be ready by tomorrow or I'll have you put to death!" The shoemaker left the palace with hanging head. His friends, who had been waiting for him, greeted him and asked how he had fared. "It's cursed I am!" he told them. "Elena the Fair will drive all us good Christians to our grave! She's ordered me to make her a dress sewn with gold and studded with precious stones, and what sort of a tailor am I! I'm sure to be put to death." "Let's have a drink or two now, friend, and then you can go to bed. Night is the mother of wisdom, don't forget."

They went to an inn and drank and made merry, and by and by the shoemaker was so drunk he could hardly stand. He dragged a keg of wine home with him and said to Prince Ivan: "Wake me tomorrow and I'll down this whole keg of wine. I want to be drunk when they chop off my head. For never in my life can I hope to make a dress like the one demanded of me." He went to bed and was soon snoring loudly, and Prince Ivan put his pipe to his lips and blew. The lame man and the one-eyed man appeared and asked him what they could do for him. "I want a dress to be made by tomorrow, and it must be as fine as the one Elena the Fair wore when she lived in Whirlwind's palace." "It shall be done!" Prince Ivan woke at dawn, and there was the dress lying on the table and sparkling so brightly that it lit up the whole room. So he went and roused the shoemaker who rubbed his eyes and said: "Have they come for me, then? Hurry and bring the wine!" "But the dress is all ready." "Is it? When did we make it?" "During the night. It was you did the cutting." "Did I? I'm that fuzzy I don't remember." And taking the dress, the shoemaker ran to the palace.

Elena the Fair gave him a large sum of money and said: "You are to build a kingdom of gold in the middle of the sea and also a bridge of gold that will connect this palace with it. The bridge is to be carpeted with the richest of velvets, beautiful trees are to grow on either side of it, and songbirds are to sit in them and sing away for all they are worth. And if it is not ready by breakfast-time tomorrow, I shall have you quartered!" The shoemaker left the palace with hanging head. "Well, how was it?" his friends asked him. "It's the end of me, I am to be quartered tomorrow. She's set me such a task that the devil himself could not cope with it!" "Now, now, let's go and have a drink and then you can go to bed. Night is the mother of wisdom, don't forget." "And why not! A man should have a little pleasure before he dies."

They went to an inn and drank much wine, and so drunk was the shoemaker by evening that his friends had to drag him home. "Goodbye, my lad!" said he to Prince Ivan. "I am to be put to death tomorrow." "Have you been set another task?" "Yes." He told Prince Ivan what it was, went to bed and was soon snoring away. And Prince Ivan went to his own room and blew upon his pipe. The lame man and the one-eyed man appeared and asked him what they could do for him. He told them what it was he wanted done, and they said: "That is no easy task, Prince Ivan, but never fear, everything will be done by tomorrow morning." Prince Ivan woke just as day broke, he looked out of the window, and lo and behold!—there stood the palace of gold flaming like fire. Prince Ivan roused the shoemaker who jumped to his feet with a start. "What is it? Have they come for me? Bring the wine, quick! I want to be put to death drunk." "But the palace has been built." "It has?" And the shoemaker glanced out of the window and gasped in wonder. "When was it built?" he asked. "Don't you remember? You and I worked very, very hard." "I must have slept so soundly I forgot all about it."

They hurried to the golden palace and found it to be full of treasures such as no one had seen or heard of before. Said Prince Ivan: "Here is a feather duster for you, Master. Go and dust the railings, and if anyone comes and asks you who lives in the palace, don't say a word but just give them this note." Off went the shoemaker and began dusting the railings, and Elena the Fair, who had just risen from bed, saw the golden bridge and hurried to tell the king about it. "Just look, Your Majesty!" she cried. "A palace of gold has been built in the middle of the sea, and a bridge too that connects it with your palace. And on either side of the bridge grow the most beautiful trees in which sit song-birds that fill the air with their music."

The king, who feared that some great warrior was about to lay seige to his kingdom, at once sent envoys to ask what it all could mean. And the shoemaker being on the bridge, the envoys addressed all their questions to him. "I know nothing, but here is a note you can take to your king," the shoemaker said. Now, in the note Prince Ivan had told his father all about everything, about how he had freed his mother and Elena the Fair and about how his elder brothers had tricked him. And he sent carriages of gold for the king and queen, asking them to pay him a visit together with Elena the Fair and her sisters. He invited his brothers too, but said that they were to travel in an ordinary peasant sled.

The king and queen and the rest did not delay but set off at once, and Prince Ivan welcomed them with great joy. The king wanted to punish his two elder sons for what they had done, but Prince Ivan pleaded with him not to and he forgave them. A great feast was then held, and Prince Ivan married Elena the Fair. He gave the Princess of the Silver Kingdom in marriage to Prince Pyotr, and the Princess of the Copper Kingdom, to Prince Vassily, and he had the shoemaker made general.

I was at the feast too, and I drank mead and wine, but all of it ran down this beard of mine.

Translated by Irina Zheleznova

Evening,
Midnight and Dawn

In a certain realm there once lived a king who had three daughters so beautiful as cannot be described. The king treasured them as the apple of his eye and had underground chambers built where they were kept like birds in a cage that the wild winds might not blow on them or the bright sun burn them with its rays. One day the three Princesses read in a book about the wonders of the great wide world, and when the king came to pay them a visit, they began pleading with him with tears in their eyes to let them out of their chambers. "Please, Father, you who are our king and ruler, let us out for a walk in the green garden that we may see the light of day!" they said. The king tried to talk them out of it, but they would not listen to him, and the more often he entreated them to think better of it the more they badgered him and the louder they begged him to do as they wished. It could not be helped, and the king gave in.

The beautiful Princesses came out for a walk in the garden, they saw the bright sun and the trees and flowers and took great joy in being free and out in the fresh air. They ran about and played, marvelling at every blade of grass and every flower, when all of a sudden the wild wind caught them up and carried them off none knew where. Their maids and women were greatly alarmed and ran to tell the king about it, and the king at once sent his many faithful servants to all parts of the realm, promising that he who found some sign of them would be richly rewarded. But though the servants searched far and near, they came back with nothing to show for it. The king then called together the highest of his

53

courtiers and asked them if there was not one among them who would undertake to try to find his daughters. And he said that he who found them would get whichever one he chose of the three in marriage and a dowry that would make him rich for the rest of his life. He addressed the courtiers once, and they were silent; he addressed them a second time, and they said nothing; he addressed them for a third time, and they uttered not a word! The king burst into tears. "It seems I have no friends or defenders to help me in my trouble," he said. And he had it heralded throughout the realm that he was waiting for someone from among the ordinary folk to come forward and offer to find his daughters.

Now, at that selfsame time, in a certain village there lived a poor widow who had three sons, strong and fearless lads all three. They had been born on one day: the eldest son in the evening, the middle son at midnight, and the youngest son at dawn, and because of that were named Evening, Midnight and Dawn. Hearing of the call put out by the king, they asked their mother's blessing, made ready and rode off for the king's own city. They came to the palace, bowed low before the king and said: "May you prosper for many years to come, Sire! We have not come here to feast but to serve you. Allow us to go to seek the Princesses." "May good luck attend you, brave youths! What are your names?" "We are brothers, and our names are Evening, Midnight and Dawn." "Is there anything I can do for you before you go?" "We want nothing for ourselves, Sire, but do not leave our mother in her old age; help her if she should be in want." The king did as they asked. He had their mother brought to the palace to live there for as long as she desired, and he gave orders that she should share of his board and be given clothes to wear from his own coffers.

The three brothers set out on their way, they rode for a month, and another, and a third, and they came to a great and empty plain. Beyond it stretched a dense forest, and they were halfway through it when there before them they saw a little hut. They knocked at the window, but there was no reply; they came inside, and there was no one there. "Well, brothers, let us stay here awhile and rest from our journey," they said. They took off their clothes, said their prayers and went to bed, and on the following morning Dawn said to his elder brother Evening: "Midnight and I will go off to hunt, and you must stay home and prepare our dinner for us." To this Evening agreed, and there being a shed full of sheep near the hut, he slaughtered the best one he could find among them and roasted it. Then, everything being ready, he lay down on a bench for a sleep. All of a sudden there came a great thumping and banging, the door opened, and a bearded old man the size of a thumb stepped into the hut looking glum as glum. "How dared you play the master in my house, how dared you slaughter my sheep!" he cried. "First grow a wee bit so a man can tell you from a bug!" Evening said. "You don't want me to drown you in a spoonful of soup, do you!" The little old man became angrier still. "I'm small but bold and can knock you out cold!" he cried. And grabbing a crust of bread, he began hitting Evening over the head with it and gave him such a walloping that he was all but dead by the time he got through with him. Then he thrust him under the bench, ate up the roasted sheep and went

54

away. And as for Evening, he came to after a while, tied a rag round his head and lay there moaning. The two brothers came back, and, seeing him in so sorry a state, asked what had happened. "Well, you see, brothers, I lit the oven and got such a terrible headache from the heat that I lay around all day in a half-swoon and could not cook anything."

On the following day Dawn and Evening went off to hunt, and they left Midnight at home to prepare the dinner.

Midnight lit the oven, slaughtered the fattest sheep he could find in the shed and, having roasted it, lay down on the bench for a sleep.

All of a sudden there was a great thumping and banging, and a little old man the size of a thumb came into the hut looking glum as glum. He fell on Midnight, gave him such a walloping that he was all but dead by the time he was through with him, and, having eaten the roasted sheep, went away. And Midnight tied a rag round his head and lay moaning under the bench. Dawn and Evening came back, and Dawn asked him what had happened to him. "I lit the oven and got such a headache from the fumes that I had to lie around all day and could not cook anything," Midnight said.

On the third day the two elder brothers went off to hunt, and Dawn stayed home. He slaughtered the best sheep he could find in the shed, skinned and roasted it, and, this done, lay down on the bench for a sleep.

All of a sudden there was a great thumping and banging, and a little old man the size of a thumb came into the yard looking glum as glum. He had a whole stack of hay on his head and a large tub of water in his hands, and having set the tub of water down on the ground and strewn the hay over the yard, began counting the sheep. Seeing that one sheep was missing, he flew into a temper, ran into the hut, threw himself at Dawn and gave him a sharp knock on the head. But Dawn jumped up, clutched the little old man by the beard and began dragging him over the floor, saying as he did so, "Look before you leap if it's whole you would keep!"

"Have mercy on me, brave youth!" cried the little old man. "Spare my life and let me go!" But Dawn dragged him out into the yard and up to a pillar of oak, and, using a wedge of iron, stuck his beard into a split in the wood. Then he came back into the hut and sat there waiting for his brothers. The brothers were soon back and they marvelled to see him unharmed. "Come out into the yard with me, brothers, and you'll see your 'headache'," said Dawn with a laugh. They came out into the yard, but the little old man was gone, and all they saw was a part of his beard sticking out from the split and a trail of blood on the ground.

The trail led the brothers to a deep pit, and Dawn went to the forest, stripped some bark off a tree, made a rope out of it and told Evening and Midnight to let him down into the pit on it. This they did, and, finding that he was in the netherworld, Dawn untied himself and set off along a road that stretched before him and led he knew not where. He walked and he walked, and there before him was a palace of copper. He stepped inside, and the youngest of the Princesses, a maid as lovely as a flower, came toward him. "Is it of your own free will or at another's bidding that you have come here, brave youth?" she asked. "It was your

56

father who sent me to seek you and your sisters," Dawn told her. The Princess at once seated him at a table, dined and wined him and then gave him a phial of strong water. "Here, drink the water, and it will make you very, very strong," said she. Dawn drank the water and at once felt himself to be filled with great strength. "Now I can get the better of anyone!" said he to himself.

All of a sudden a wild wind began to blow, and the Princess was frightened. "The three-headed dragon is coming!" she cried, and she took Dawn by the hand and hid him in her chamber. The dragon now came flying up, and he struck the ground and turned into a man. "I smell Russian flesh!" he cried. "Is anyone here?" "How could there be!" the Princess said. "You have been flying over Russ and must have brought the smell of Russian flesh with you." The dragon asked her to give him food and drink, and she brought in a plate of food and a goblet of wine, and, first having added sleeping powder to the wine, offered it to him. The dragon ate and drank, and, feeling very sleepy, placed his head on the Princess's lap and fell fast asleep. The Princess at once called Dawn, who came out of his hiding-place and smote off all of the dragon's three heads with one stroke of his sword. He then made up a fire, burnt the dragon's body and strewed the ashes over the plain.

"And now I must bid you goodbye, Princess," said Dawn, "for I am off to seek your sisters. But I will come back for you as soon as I find them."

He set off on his way, he walked and he walked, and there before him rose a silver palace in which the middle sister was kept captive by a six-headed dragon. Dawn killed the dragon, freed the Princess and went on. Whether a short or a long time passed nobody knows, but he came at last to a palace of gold where the eldest Princess was kept captive by a twelve-headed dragon. He killed the dragon, and the Princess was overjoyed and prepared to set out for home. She came out into the courtyard and waved a red kerchief, and the kingdom of gold turned into a golden egg. This she put in her pocket and went with Dawn to where he had left her sisters. Then after the middle princess had turned her kingdom into a silver egg and the younger sister had turned hers into a copper egg, the four of them made for the bottom of the pit. Evening and Midnight dragged Dawn and the three princesses out of the pit, and they all went back together to their own realm. The princesses sent the eggs rolling over the plain, and at once the three kingdoms, one of copper, one of silver and one of gold, appeared before them. They came to the palace, and so happy was the king as cannot be told! He married his youngest daughter to Dawn, his middle daughter to Evening, and his eldest daughter to Midnight, and he made Dawn his heir.

Translated by Irina Zheleznova

Shabarsha

How about a nice story, ladies and gents? A fairy story with lots of weird and wonderful happenings and that rogue to end all rogues, Shabarsha, who never does things by halves, and no mistake! Shabarsha hired himself out, but it was a real bad harvest that year. His master racked his brains about how to drive away care, keep the wolf from the door and get hold of some cash. "Do not worry, master!" Shabarsha said to him. "Just give me the day, and I'll find a way!" And off he went to the mill pond. "I'll catch some fish," he thought, "then sell it and get some money! Bother, I haven't got any twine for the hook... Never mind, I'll made some." He asked the miller for some hemp, sat down on the bank and began to make twine.

While he was working a little boy in a black jacket and red cap jumped out of the water onto the bank. "What are you doing, uncle?" he asked. "Making some twine." "What for?" "I'm going to clean up the pond and pull you devils out of the water." "Oh, no! Wait a moment, I'll go and tell my grandad." The little devil dived into the water, and Shabarsha went on with his work. "Ha, ha," he thought, "I'll play a trick on you, you wicked crew, and make you give me all your gold and silver." And Shabarsha dug a deep hole and placed his cap upside down over it. But the crafty fellow had cut the top off. "Shabarsha! Hey, Shabarsha! Grandad says I must strike a bargain with you. What will you take to leave us in peace?" "Fill this cap here with gold and silver".

The devil boy dived back into the water and then returned. "Grandad says that first you and I must have a wrestling match." "How can a puny stripling like you wrestle with me! You couldn't even take on my middle brother Bruin." "Where is he, this Bruin of yours?" "Over there, resting in that hollow under a bush." "How can I get him to wrestle?" "Just give him a dig in the ribs. He'll get up alright then." The devil boy went to the hollow, found the bear and poked him in the ribs with a stick. Bruin reared up on his hind legs and hugged the devil boy so hard that his ribs cracked. He struggled free from the bear's clutches and fled back to the old man in the pond. "Grandad!" he squealed in terror, "Shabarsha's middle brother called Bruin wrestled with me and made my ribs crack! What would have happened if I'd wrestled with Shabarsha himself?" "Hmm. Go back and have a race with Shabarsha. See who comes first."

So the boy in the red cap went back to Shabarsha and told him what his grandad had said. "You race against me! Why, even my little brother Harry Hare would leave you miles behind!" "Where is your brother, Harry Hare?" "Over there, lying in the grass, having a rest. Go up and tickle his ear—he'll race with you alright then." The devil boy ran up to Harry Hare and tickled his ear. Off the hare shot like lightning, leaving the boy far behind. "Stop, stop, Harry Hare. Wait for me. Oh dear, he's gone!" "I was going to race like the winds, grandad," he explained to the water demon. "But I never had a chance, and it wasn't Shabarsha himself, just his young brother!" "Hmm," muttered the old man, frowning darkly. "Go and have a whistling contest with Shabarsha. See who can whistle the loudest."

"Shabarsha! Hey, Shabarsha! Grandad says we must see who can whistle the loudest." "Alright, you whistle first." The devil boy whistled so loudly that Shabarsha could hardly keep on his feet, and the leaves fell off the trees. "Not bad," said Shabarsha, "but not as good as me! When I whistle you'll be knocked off your feet and your eardrums will split. So lie face down on the ground and put your hands over your ears." The devil boy lay face down and covered his ears with his hands. Shabarsha took a heavy stick, brought it down with all his might on the devil boy's neck, and whistled. "Oh, grandad, grandad! Shabarsha gave such a whistle that I saw stars before my eyes. I could hardly get up from the ground, and all the bones in my neck and back felt broken." "Ho, you're not very strong, my lad! Go and get my iron cudgel from the reeds and see which of you can toss it higher."

The devil boy found the cudgel, heaved it onto his shoulder and went to Shabarsha. "Shabarsha, grandad told me to have one more try. Let's see which of us can toss this cudgel highest into the air." "Alright, you toss first and I'll watch." The devil boy tossed the cudgel up, and it flew higher and higher until it was only a tiny dot in the sky. They had to wait an age for it to come down again. Then Shabarsha picked it up. Phew, what a weight! He leaned on it and gazed up at the sky. "I'm waiting for that black cloud to get nearer. I'll throw the cudgel up to it. My brother the blacksmith is up there and he could do with a nice bit of iron like this." "Oh, no, Shabarsha! Don't throw the cudgel up to the cloud. Grandad will be angry!" The devil boy snatched the cudgel and dived back to his grandfather.

When his grandfather heard that Shabarsha had almost thrown his cudgel away, he got such a fright that he ordered the money to be fetched from the pond and given to Shabarsha. The devil boy kept pouring money into the cap, but still it was not full. "Shabarsha's got a mighty strange cap, grandad. I keep filling it with gold and silver, but it's still empty. You have only one more chest left now." "Take that up too quickly. Is he getting the twine ready?" "Yes, grandad!" "Hurry up then." There was nothing for it. The devil boy took his grandfather's last precious chest and poured the coins into Shabarsha's cap, until at last it was full! Ever since that day Shabarsha has lived in clover. I was asked round to drink mead and beer with him, but I did not go. They say the mead was bitter, and the beer cloudy. So what might be the meaning of that, eh?

Translated by Kathleen Cook

Marya Morevna

In a certain kingdom, in a certain realm there once lived a king and a queen with their son, Prince Ivan, and their three daughters, Princess Marya, Princess Olga and Princess Anna. The time came for the mother and father to die, and as they lay on their death-bed they told their son not to keep his sisters long unwed but to marry them off to whoever came to woo them first. The king and queen died, Prince Ivan laid them to rest, and, his heart filled with sorrow, went for a walk in their green garden with his three sisters. All of a sudden a black cloud came over the sky: a terrible storm was about to break. "Come, sisters, let us go home!" said Prince Ivan. No sooner were they back in the palace than the thunder crashed, the ceiling was rent in two, and a falcon flew into the chamber. He struck the floor, turned into a tall and handsome youth, and said: "Good morrow to you, Prince Ivan. Many a time did I come to your house as a guest, but now I come as a wooer. For I wish to ask for the hand of your sister, Princess Marya." "If my sister likes you, I'll not say nay; she can marry you, and may God bless you both!" said Prince Ivan. And Princess Marya being willing, Falcon married her and carried her off to his kingdom.

Day followed day, and hour followed hour, and a whole year went by before ever they knew it. Prince Ivan went for a walk in the green garden with his two sisters, and again a black cloud covered the sky, the lightning flared, and a fierce wind began to blow. "Come, sisters, let us go home!" said Prince Ivan. No sooner were they back in the palace than the thunder crashed, the ceiling was rent in two, and an eagle came flying in. He struck the floor and turned into a tall and handsome youth. "Good morrow to you, Prince Ivan," said he. "Many a time did I come here as a guest, but now I come as a wooer." And he asked for the hand of Princess Olga. "If Princess Olga likes you, you can have her," said Prince Ivan. "She is free to do as she chooses."

And Princess Olga being willing, Eagle married her and carried her off to his kingdom.

Another year passed, and Prince Ivan said to his youngest sister: "Come, Sister, let us take a walk in the green garden." They had a little walk, and again a black cloud covered the sky, the lightning flared, and a fierce wind began to blow. "Let us go home, Sister!" said Prince Ivan. They came home, and before they had time to sit down, the thunder crashed, the ceiling was rent in two, and a raven came flying in. He struck the floor and turned into a tall and handsome youth, more handsome even than the other two. "Many a time did I come here as a guest, but now I come as a wooer," said he. "Let me have Princess Anna in marriage." "My sister is free to do as she chooses," said Prince Ivan. "If she likes you, she can marry you." And Princess Anna being willing, Raven married her and carried her off to his kingdom.

Prince Ivan was left all by himself. He lived alone for a whole year, and he missed his sisters very much. "I think I'll go and look up my sisters," said he. Off he set from home, he rode and he rode, and by and by he came to a field where a whole host of warriors lay routed and dead.

"If there is a man left alive among you, let him answer me!" Prince Ivan called out. "For I wish to know who it was that vanquished this whole mighty host." And the only living man there replied: "This whole mighty host was vanquished by Marya Morevna, the fairest of queens." Prince Ivan rode on. He came upon a number of white tents set up in a field, and there, coming out to meet him, was Marya Morevna, the fairest of queens. "Good morrow, Prince," said she. "Whither bound? Do you come of your own free will or at another's bidding?" Said Prince Ivan in reply: "Men who are bold of spirit never go anywhere but of their own free will." "Well, if you are in no great haste, then be my guest and bide in my tent awhile." This Prince Ivan was pleased to do. For two days and two nights he was Marya Morevna's guest, and so well did they like one another that they became man and wife, and Marya Morevna, the fairest of queens, took Prince Ivan with her to her kingdom.

They lived together for a time, but then came a day when Marya Morevna bethought her of setting out again for the wars. She left her palace and everything in it in Prince Ivan's care, and, showing him a room the door to which was locked and bolted, said: "You must look after everytning and are free to enter any room in this palace save this one!" But Prince Ivan's curiosity got the better of him, and no sooner had Marya Morevna left than he hurried to the room and unlocked the door. He looked in, and whom should he see hanging there, chained to the wall with twelve chains, but Koshchei the Deathless. Said Koshchei the Deathless in pleading tones: "Take pity on me, Prince Ivan, give me some water to drink. For ten years have I been held here and great have been my torments. I have had no food and nothing to drink, and my throat is all dry and parched."

63

Prince Ivan gave him a whole pailful of water to drink, and Koshchei drank it and began pleading for more. "One pail is not enough, do let me have another," he begged. Prince Ivan gave him a second pail of water, and Koshchei gulped it down and asked for a third. But when he had finished his third pailful he got back all of his strength, and, shaking his chains, broke all twelve of them. "Thank you, Prince Ivan," said he. "Now you will never see Marya Morevna, no more than you can see your own ears."

He flew out of the window like a whirlwind, caught up Marya Morevna, the fairest of queens, and carried her off with him. Prince Ivan wept long and bitterly, and then he made ready and set off in search of Marya Morevna. "Come what may, I shall find her!" said he.

A day passed, and another, and at dawn on the third day Prince Ivan saw a beautiful palace before him. Beside the palace there grew an oak and on its bough there sat a falcon. The falcon flew off the oak, struck the ground and turned into a handsome youth. "Ah, my own dear brother-in-law, I am indeed glad to see you!" he cried. "How have you been?" And now Princess Marya came hurrying out of the palace. She welcomed Prince Ivan joyously, asked after his health and told him how she lived and fared. Prince Ivan spent three days with them and then he said: "I cannot stay with you longer. I must go to seek my wife, Marya Morevna, the fairest of queens." "It won't be easy to find her," Falcon told him. "Leave your silver spoon here just in case. We will look at it and think of you." Prince Ivan left his silver spoon with Falcon and set off on his way.

He rode for a day, and another day, and at dawn on the third day, standing before him he saw a palace which was even more beautiful than Falcon's. Beside the palace there grew an oak and on its bough there sat an eagle. The eagle flew off the oak, struck the ground and turned into a handsome youth. "Come, Princess Olga, get up, for our own dear brother is here!" he cried. Princess Olga came running out of the palace. She embraced Prince Ivan, asked after his health and told him how she lived and fared. Prince Ivan spent three days with them and then he said: "I cannot stay with you longer. I must go to seek my wife, Marya Morevna, the fairest of queens." "It will not be easy to find her," said Eagle. "Leave your silver fork with us. We will look at it and think of you." So Prince Ivan left his silver fork with them and set off on his way.

He rode for a day, and another day, and at dawn on the third day, standing before him, he saw a palace which far surpassed the first two in beauty and splendour. Beside the palace there grew an oak and on its bough there sat a raven. The raven flew off the oak, struck the ground and turned into a handsome youth. "Come, Princess Anna, make haste and join me, for our own dear brother is here!" he cried. Princess Anna came running out of the palace. She greeted Prince Ivan joyously, embraced and kissed him, asked after his health and told him how she lived and fared. Prince Ivan spent three days with them and then he said: "Farewell, I must go to seek my wife Marya Morevna, the fairest of queens." "It will not be easy to find her," said Raven. "Leave your silver snuff-box with us.

We will look at it and think of you." Prince Ivan gave Raven his silver snuff-box, and, taking leave of him and Princess Anna, set off on his way.

A day passed, and another day, but it was only on the third day that he found Marya Morevna. Seeing him, Marya Morevna threw her arms around Prince Ivan, burst into tears and said: "Ah, Prince Ivan, why did you not listen to me? Why did you let out Koshchei the Deathless?" "Forgive me, Marya Morevna, and hold no grudge against me," said Prince Ivan. "Come away with me while Koschei the Deathless is nowhere to be seen and perhaps he will not overtake us." And the two of them made ready for the journey and rode away together. Now, Koshchei the Deathless was out hunting. It was evening by the time he turned his way homewards, and as he rode along his horse stumbled under him. "Why do you stumble, you old bag of bones?" he asked. "Is it that you sense some misfortune?" Said the horse in reply: "Prince Ivan has been in your house and he has carried off Marya Morevna." "Can we catch them up?" "If we were to sow some wheat, wait till it ripened, reap and thresh it and grind in into flour, bake five ovenfuls of bread and not go after them till we had eaten it all up, we should still catch them up." So Koshchei the Deathless sent his horse into a gallop, and he caught up Prince Ivan. "I forgive you this first time," said he, "for you were kind to me and gave me water to drink, and perhaps I'll forgive you a second time. But if you dare to go against me a third time, beware, for I will hack you to pieces!" He took Marya Morevna away from him and rode away with her, and Prince Ivan sat down on a stone by the wayside and wept and sorrowed. Then, drying his tears, he went back again for Marya Morevna.

Koshchei the Deathless was away from home. "Come with me, Marya Morevna," said Prince Ivan. "Ah, Prince Ivan, Koshchei will overtake us again!" "Let him! We shall at least have spent an hour or two together." So the two of them made ready for the journey and away they rode. By and by Koshchei the Deathless turned his way homewards. He rode along, and his horse stumbled under him. "You old bag of bones you, why do you stumble? Is it that you sense some misfortune?" he asked. "Prince Ivan has been in your house and has carried off Marya Morevna." "Can we catch them up?" "If we were to sow some barley, wait till it ripened, reap and thresh it, brew beer out of it, drink till we were drunk and not go after them till we had slept it off, we should still catch them up." So Koshchei the Deathless put his horse into a gallop, and he caught up Prince Ivan. "I told you you would no more see Marya Morevna than your own ears," he said. And he took her away from Prince Ivan and carried her off with him.

Prince Ivan was left alone, he wept and sorrowed, and then he went back again for Marya Morevna. And Koshchei the Deathless happened to be away from home as before. "Come with me, Marya Morevna!" said Prince Ivan. "Ah, Prince Ivan, Koshchei will overtake us and hack you to pieces!" "Let him! I cannot live without you." So the two of them made ready for the journey and away they rode. By and by Koshchei the Deathless turned his way homewards. He rode along, and his horse stumbled under him. "Why do you stumble? Is it that you sense some misfortune?" he asked. "Prince Ivan has been in your house and has carried off

Marya Morevna." Off Koshchei galloped after Prince Ivan, he caught him up, hacked him to pieces, put the pieces in a tarred barrel, bound the barrel with iron hoops and cast it in the blue sea. And he carried Marya Morevna off with him again.

Now, at this selfsame time the silver things Prince Ivan had left with his brothers-in-law lost their lustre and turned dark. "Prince Ivan must have met with some misfortune," said the brothers-in-law. So down Eagle dropped to the blue sea, seized the barrel and carried it out on to the shore. Falcon flew for some living water, and Raven for some dead water, and the two of them came flying back to where Eagle was waiting for them. They broke the barrel, took out the pieces into which Prince Ivan's body had been hacked, washed them and put them all together again properly. Raven sprinkled the pieces with dead water, and they grew fast to one another, and then Falcon sprayed them with living water, and Prince Ivan started and rose to his feet. "Ah, what a long sleep I have had!" he said. "You would have slept longer if it were not for us," his brothers-in-law told him. "And now come and be our guest." "No, my brothers, I must go and seek Marya Morevna."

Back he went again to Koshchei's palace, and it was there he found her. "Ask Koshchei where it was he got himself such a fine horse," he said to her. Marya Morevna bided her time and then she asked Koshchei the Deathless about his horse. Said Koshchei the Deathless: "Beyond the thrice-nine lands, in the thrice-ten kingdom there lives Baba-Yaga the Witch. Her house stands in a forest beyond the Flaming River, and she has many fine mares, among them one on which she flies round the world every day. I tended them for three days, and she gave me a foal in reward." "How did you manage to cross the Flaming River?" "With the help of my magic kerchief. I have only to wave it three times with my right hand, and a bridge so tall will rise before me that no flames can reach it." Marya Morevna heard him out and passed on every word to Prince Ivan. And she carried off Koshchei's magic kerchief and gave it to him.

Prince Ivan crossed the Flaming River and made for Baba-Yaga's house. On and on he walked for a long time, and he had to do without food or drink. By and by he came upon a strange bird and her brood of chicks. "I think I shall eat one of the chicks," said he. "Please, Prince Ivan, do not touch my chicks," said the bird in pleading tones. "Who knows but you may have need of me some day!" Prince Ivan walked on, and he came upon a bee-hive. "I think I shall take some honey," said he. "Do not touch my honey, Prince Ivan," said the bee queen. "Who knows but you may have need of me some day!" Prince Ivan walked on, and whom should he see coming toward him but a lioness and her cub. "I think I'll eat the cub," said Prince Ivan. "I'm weak with hunger." "Please, Prince Ivan, do not touch my cub," said the lioness in pleading tones. "Who knows but you may have need of me some day!" "Very well, then, let it be as you ask."

He walked on, as hungry as ever, and he came to Baba-Yaga's house. Stuck into the ground all around it were twelve poles, all save one of them crowned with human heads. "Good morrow, Grandma!" said Prince Ivan to Baba-Yaga. "Good morrow to you, Prince Ivan! What brings you here?" "I have come to serve you, and I hope to get one of your fine steeds in reward." "So be it, Prince Ivan! It is not for a year but for only three days that you must serve me. If you keep my mares safe you shall have a fine steed in reward. If you don't, then your head will crown the last pole of the twelve, and you'll have no one but yourself to blame." To this Prince Ivan agreed, and Baba-Yaga gave him food and drink and told him to set to work. Prince Ivan drove the mares to pasture, but no sooner had he done so than they lifted their tails and galloped off across the meadows. And before he had had time to bat an eye they were out of sight. Prince Ivan wept and sorrowed, and then he sat down on a stone and fell asleep. The sun had already set beyond the forest when the bird whose chick he had spared came flying up to him. "Wake up, Prince Ivan!" she called. "The mares are all back in their stall." Prince Ivan went home, and there was Baba-Yaga making a great to-do and shouting at her mares. "Why did you come back home?" she demanded of them. "What else could we do! Birds from all over the world came flying at us and nearly pecked out our eyes." "Well, don't run over the meadows tomorrow but hide in the forests."

Prince Ivan slept the night through and woke to see Baba-Yaga standing over him. "It is morning and time for you to pasture the mares," said she. "And if you should lose even one of them your head shall crown the last pole of the twelve." Prince Ivan drove the mares to pasture, and they at once lifted their tails and ran away deep into the forests. He wept and he sorrowed and then he sat down on a stone and fell asleep. The sun had already sunk when the lioness came running up to him. "Wake up, Prince Ivan," she cried. "The mares are all back in the stall." Prince Ivan went home, and there was Baba-Yaga making a great to-do and shouting at the mares. "Why did you come back home!" she demanded of them. "What else could we do! The fiercest beasts from all over the world set upon us and nearly tore us to pieces." "Well, then, you had better hid in the blue sea tomorrow."

Prince Ivan slept the night through, and in the morning Baba-Yaga sent him off to pasture her mares again. "If you lose even one of them your head shall crown the last pole of the twelve," said she. Prince Ivan drove the mares to pasture, and they at once lifted their tails and vanished from sight. Into the blue sea they ran and they stood up to their necks in the water. Prince Ivan sat down on a stone. He wept and sorrowed and then fell asleep. The sun had already sunk beyond the forest when the bee queen came flying up to him. "Get up, Prince Ivan!" she cried. "The mares are all back in their stalls. Only mind, when you get back to the house, do not let Baba-Yaga see you but go to the stable and hide behind the crib. There is a mangy colt there wallowing in the dung. Lead him out in the deep of night and ride away."

Prince Ivan made his way to Baba-Yaga's house. He stole into the stable and lay down behind the crib, and there was Baba-Yaga making a great to-do and shouting at her mares. "Why did you come back home?" she demanded of them. "What else could we do! Swarms of bees came flying at us and they stung us all over."

Baba-Yaga went to bed and to sleep, and on the stroke of midnight Prince Ivan saddled the mangiest of her colts, sprang on his back and rode to the Flaming River. And no sooner was he there than he waved his magic kerchief thrice with his right hand, and lo!—there before him, spanning the river, rose a fine, tall bridge. Prince Ivan rode across, he waved his kerchief twice with his left hand, and the fine tall bridge turned into a narrow, low one. Morning came, Baba-Yaga woke, and, seeing that her colt was gone, rushed off in pursuit. Like the wind she flew in her iron mortar, using her pestle for a whip and sweeping the tracks away with her broom.

She flew up to the Flaming River, and, seeing the bridge, started off across it. But just as she got to the middle of it, the bridge broke down under her, and she fell into the water and drowned.

Prince Ivan pastured his colt in the lush green meadows, and when the colt grew up to be a strong and handsome steed, he saddled him and made for the house of Koshshei the Deathless. Seeing him, Marya Morevna came running out of the house and threw her arms round him. "How did you come back to life?" she asked him. "God must have been watching over you." Prince Ivan told her of all that had passed. "And now you must come away with me," he said. "I'm afraid, Prince Ivan! If Koshchei overtakes us he'll hack you to pieces again." "He'll not overtake us this time, for my horse flies like the wind." And they mounted the horse and rode away. By and by, Koshchei the Deathless, who had been out hunting, turned his way homewards. On he rode, and his horse stumbled under him. "Why do you stumble, you old bag of bones?" he asked him. "Is it that you sense some misfortune?" "Prince Ivan has been in your house and has carried off Marya Morevna." "Can we catch them up?" "God knows! For now Prince Ivan has a house as fine as I am or finer." "That isn't going to stop me," said Koshchei the Deathless. "I'll go after them!" Whether a short or a long time passed, nobody knows, but he caught up Prince Ivan, and, jumping to the ground, was about to pierce him with his sword. But before he could do it, Prince Ivan's horse struck him with his hoof with all his might and smashed his head, and Prince Ivan finished him off with his cudgel. After that Prince Ivan brought a heap of firewood and made a fire. He burnt the body of Koshchei the Deathless and cast his ashes into the wind.

Marya Morevna got on Koshchei's horse and Prince Ivan on his own, and away they rode. First they went to see Raven, then Falcon and then Eagle, and they were welcomed with joy by all three. "Ah, Prince Ivan, we had lost all hope of ever seeing you!" they said. "But greatly as you have suffered, it was worth it. For if you searched the world over you would never find a bride as lovely as Marya Morevna!" Prince Ivan and Marya Morevna feasted and made merry, and then they went back to their own kingdom. And there they lived in good health and good cheer for many a long and prosperous year: they never knew hunger, they never knew need, and they drank their fill of ale and of mead.

Translated by Irina Zheleznova

King Ivan and Bely, the Warrior of the Plains

In a certain kingdom, in a certain realm there was once a king who had three daughters and one son, Prince Ivan. The king grew old and died, and Prince Ivan was crowned king. As soon as the rulers of the neighbouring realms heard about it they mustered a great host and made war on him. King Ivan did not know what to do. Said he to his sisters: "What am I to do, my dear sisters? The rulers of the neighbouring realms have all sent out their armies against me."

"What sort of warrior are you!" the sisters said. "What have you to fear? Why, Bely, the Warrior of the Plains, has been warring with Baba-Yaga the Leg of Gold for seven years now, and he has never left his horse's back in all that time! How can you take fright without ever having seen any fighting?" King Ivan at once saddled his trusty steed, donned his armour, took his sword of steel, his great spear and his silken lash, said his prayers and rode out against his foes. He mowed down many with his sword, and many more were trampled to death by his horse, and when the whole of the enemy host was vanquished, he came back home and fell into a sound sleep. For three days and three nights he slept and only woke on the fourth day. He came out on to his balcony and glanced at the field of battle, and lo!—his foes had mustered a new and greater host against him and had drawn it up to the town's very walls.

King Ivan was much grieved and went to see his sisters. "What am I to do, my sisters?" said he. "I have vanquished one host, but now there is another and

70

bigger one at the town walls." "What sort of warrior are you!" the sisters said. "You fought for a day and a night and then slept without waking for three days and three nights. Why, Bely, the Warrior of the Plains, has been warring with Baba-Yaga the Leg of Gold for seven years, and he has never left his horse's back in all that time!" King Ivan took these words sorely to heart. He hurried to his stables of white stone, saddled his trusty steed, donned his armour, hung a sword of steel at his side, took a great spear in one hand and a silken lash in the other, said his prayers and rode out against his foes. Not a falcon was it swooping down on a herd of swans but King Ivan coming at the enemy host. Many were the warriors he mowed down and many more did his horse trample to death. He vanquished the whole of the enemy host, came back home and fell into a sound sleep. For six days and six nights he slept and only woke on the seventh day. He came out on to his balcony and looked at the field of battle, and lo!—his foes had mustered an even greater host and laid siege to the town.

King Ivan went to see his sisters. "What am I to do, my dear sisters?" said he. "I have vanquished two enemy hosts, but a third and even bigger one is at our walls." "What sort of warrior are you!" the sisters said. "You fought for a day and a night and slept for six days and six nights. Why, Bely, the Warrior of the Plains, has been warring with Baba-Yaga the Leg of Gold for seven years now, and he has never left his horse's back or had a rest in all that time!" King Ivan took these words sorely to heart. He hurried to his stables of white stone, saddled his trusty steed, donned his armour, hung a sword of steel at his side, took a great spear in one hand and a silken lash in the other, said his prayers and rode out against his foes. Not a falcon was it swooping down on a herd of swans but King Ivan coming at the enemy host. Many were the warriors he mowed down and meny more did his horse trample to death. He vanquished the whole of the enemy host, came back home and fell into a sound sleep. For nine days and nine nights he slept and only woke on the tenth day. He called all his nobles and councillors and said to them: "Hear me, my nobles and councillors! I have made up my mind to set off for distant lands and see Bely, the warrior of the Plains, for myself. And I leave you here to rule the realm in my stead and to judge all men fairly." He bade his sisters goodbye, mounted his horse and set out on his way.

Whether a short or a long time passed nobody knows, but he came at last to a dark forest where stood a little hut. An old man lived in the hut, and King Ivan came inside and greeted him. "Good morrow, old man!" said he. "Good morrow to you, King Ivan!" the old man said. "Whither are you bound"? "I am seeking Bely, the Warrior of the Plains. Do you know where he is to be found?" "No, I don't. But wait. I will call my faithful servants and ask them about it." The old man stepped out on to the porch, put a silver trumpet to his lips and blew, and all of a sudden flocks of birds came flying up to him from all sides. There were countless numbers of them, and they covered the whole of the sky like a great black cloud. The old man gave a loud whistle and said in a loud voice: "Hear me, O birds, hear me, my faithful servants! Have you ever seen or heard of Bely, the

Warrior of the Plains?" "No! Never have we seen him and never have we heard of him!" "Well, then, King Ivan," the old man said, "you had better go to see my elder brother and perhaps he can tell you what you want to know. Here, take this ball of thread and throw it before you, and wherever it rolls there must you go." King Ivan did as he was told. He mounted his horse, sent the ball of thread rolling before him and rode after it.

The forest grew darker and darker, and by and by he rode up to a little hut and came inside. An old man with hair as white as snow sat there, and he bowed to him and said: "Good morrow, old man!" "Good morrow to you, King Ivan!" the old man said. "Whither are you bound?" "I am seeking Bely, the Warrior of the Plains. Do you know where he is to be found?" "Bide here awhile. I will call together my faithful servants and ask them about it." The old man stepped out on to the porch, put a silver trumpet to his lips and blew, and all of a sudden all of the beasts of the field and the forest came running up to him. The old man gave a loud whistle and he said in a loud voice: "Hear me, O beasts of the field and the forest, hear me, my faithful servants! Have you ever seen or heard of Bely, the Warrior of the Plains?" "No," said they. "Never have we seen him and never have we heard of him." "Come, now, look about you! Perhaps not all of you are here?" The beasts looked about them and saw that the one-eyed she-wolf was not there. The old man bade them fetch her, and the she-wolf was soon brought before him. "Tell me, one-eyed she-wolf," said the old man, "have you ever seen Bely, the Warrior of the Plains?" "I know him well, for I am ever at his side," the she-wolf told him. "He wars with his enemies and kills many, and I eat of their flesh." "Where is he now?" "On a high mound in the open field, asleep in his tent. He was fighting Baba-Yaga the Leg of Gold, and after the battle was over, fell into a sound sleep. And he will not wake for twelve days and twelve nights." "Take King Ivan to him, one-eyed she-wolf!" The one-eyed she-wolf did as she was told. Off she set at a run on her way and King Ivan rode after her.

He rode up to a great mound with a tent on top of it, jumped down from his horse's back and came inside the tent, and there, lying fast asleep, was Bely, the Warrior of the Plains. "My sisters told me that Bely, the Warrior of the Plains, wars with his enemies without ever taking a rest, but here he is fast asleep and not about to wake," King Ivan said to himself. "So why don't I have a sleep too!" And he stretched himself out by Bely's side. Now, that same moment a little bird came flying into the tent. It flutterd about near Bely's head and cried: "Come, wake up, Bely, the Warrior of the Plains, and put my brother, King Ivan, to death. For if you don't, he will kill you!" Hearing it, King Ivan sprang to his feet, caught the bird and tore off its right leg. This done, he threw the bird out of the tent and lay down beside Bely, the Warrior of the Plains, again. But he was not yet asleep when a second bird came flying in. It fluttered about near Bely's head and cried: "Come, wake up, Bely, the Warrior of the Plains, and put my brother, King Ivan, to death. For if you don't, he will kill you!" At this King Ivan sprang to his feet, caught the bird, tore off its right wing, threw the bird out of the tent and lay down in the selfsame place again. By and by a third bird came flying in. It fluttered about near Bely and cried: "Come, wake up, Bely, the Warrior of the Plains, and put my brother, King Ivan, to death. For if you don't, he will kill you!" At this King Ivan sprang to his feet, caught the bird and tore off its beak. He flung the bird out of the tent and himself lay down and fell fast asleep again.

The twelve days and twelve nights were up, and Bely, the Warrior of the Plains, woke and saw a mighty warrior, one he did not know, lying beside him. He pulled out his sharp sword and was about to kill him, but stopped himself in time. "No," said he to himself. "He found me here asleep and never touched me, so no honour will attach to me if I kill him. A man asleep is like one dead. I had better wake him." He woke King Ivan and said to him: "Speak and tell me what your name is, whether you are a good man or a wicked one, and what it was that brought you here." "My name is King Ivan, and I came here to see you and to test your strength." "You are bold, King Ivan! You came into my tent and lay down beside me without my permission. That is enough for me to want to do away with you!" "Wait, Bely, the Warrior of the Plains, don't say that you can leap across a ditch before doing it—you may yet stumble. You have two hands, it's true, but then so have I!"

They mounted their trusty steeds, sent them into a gallop and clashed with each other with such force that their spears broke to pieces and their steeds fell to their knees. King Ivan sent Bely, the Warrior of the Plains, flying from his saddle, and, holding his sword over him, was about to kill him, but Bely said to him in pleading tones: "Have mercy, King Ivan! Spare my life, and I will be as a younger brother to you and will honour and esteem you as I would my own father." And King Ivan took him by the hand, helped him to his feet and put his arms lovingly around him. "I have heard, my brother, that you have been warring with Baba-Yaga the Leg of Gold for seven years. What is the reason for this?" "It is that Baba-Yaga has a beautiful daughter whom I wish to wed and whom she refuses to give me in marriage." "What are friends for if they will not help one another!" said King Ivan. "Let us fight Baba-Yaga together!"

They got on their horses and rode out into the open field, and there was Baba-Yaga waiting to meet them with her warrior host. Not two falcons were these swooping down on a flock of pigeons but two mighty warriors attacking their foes! They mowed down many with their swords and many more were trampled to death by their horses. Seeing thousands of her warriors lying there dead, Baba-Yaga fled from the field of battle, but King Ivan saw her and galloped after her. He had nearly caught her up when she came to a deep pit, and, lifting the heavy slab of iron that covered it, vanished underground. King Ivan and Bely, the Warrior of the Plains, bought a large number of oxen. They slaughtered and skinned them, cut up the skins into thongs and then plaited them together, making a rope so long that it could reach as far as the netherworld. Said King

Ivan to Bely, the Warrior of the Plains: "Hurry and let me down into the pit, but do not pull up the rope till I tug at it at the other end!" Bely, the Warrior of the Plains, let him down to the bottom of the pit, and King Ivan looked about him and went to seek Baba-Yaga.

He walked and he walked and he saw a house with a latticed door and some clothes-makers sitting behind it. "What are you doing there?" he asked them. "Making a warrior host for Baba-Yaga the Leg of Gold, King Ivan." "How do you go about it?" "Here's how. We take a piece of cloth and run it through with a needle, the piece turns into a man, the man mounts his horse, and away he rides to fight Bely, the Warrior of the Plains." "Ah, well, what you do you do quickly but not well! Come out here and line up before me, and I will show you how to make things properly." They lined up before him, and King Ivan waved his sword, smote off their heads with one stroke and went on. He walked and he walked, and he saw a house with a latticed door and some shoemakers sitting behind it. "What are you doing there?" he asked them. "Making a warrior host for Baba-Yaga the Leg of Gold." "How do you go about it?" "Here's how. We take a piece of leather and pierce it with an awl, the piece turns into a man, the man mounts a horse, and away he rides to fight Bely, the Warrior of the Plains!" "Ah, well, my good fellows, what you do you do quickly but not well. Come out and line up before me, and I will show you how to make things properly." They lined up before him, and King Ivan waved his sword, smote off their heads and walked on.

Whether a short or a long time passed nobody knows, but he came to a large and beautiful town. There was a palace there and at the window sat a maid as fair as cannot be told! She saw the young king, she liked his dark hair and eyes, his sable-black brows and his manly bearing, and she called to him and asked him to come in. King Ivan did so and she bade him tell her where he was going and what his errand was. "I am seeking Baba-Yaga the Leg of Gold," King Ivan said. "Well, I am Baba-Yaga's daughter," said the maid. "My mother is in her house sound asleep and will not wake for twelve days and twelve nights." And she led King Ivan to the town gate and showed him the road he was to follow if he wanted to get to her mother's house. King Ivan found the house and Baba-Yaga in it snoring away on her bed, and he waved his sword and smote off her head. And as it rolled across the floor it said: "Strike me again, King Ivan!" "A good warrior need strike but once!" King Ivan replied. He came back to the palace where lived Baba-Yaga's daughter and sat down beside her at an oaken table spread with a silk-sewn cloth. He ate and drank his fill and then asked the maid if she had ever heard of a man stronger than he was and a maid fairer than she. "Ah, King Ivan, I may be fair, but I know of one who is more fair by far!" the maid said. "She is a princess whom a dragon is keeping captive in his palace beyond the thrice-nine lands, in the thrice-ten kingdom."

King Ivan took the maid by the hand and led her to the place where hung the rope made of ox skins. He wound the rope tightly round her and round himself too and tugged at it, signalling Bely, the Warrior of the Plains, to haul them up.

And Bely took hold of the rope and pulled at it till he had both of them safely beside him. "I am glad to see you, Bely, Warrior of the Plains!" King Ivan said. "Here is a maid who will make you a fine wife, and may you two never grieve and never brood but always he in a cheery mood! And as for me, I am off for the Dragon's kingdom!" He mounted his trusty steed, bade Bely, the Warrior of the Plians, and his bride goodbye and set off on his way beyond the thrice-nine lands. Whether a short or a long time passed nobody knows, for a tale is quick in the telling but a deed is slow in the doing, but he came at last to the Dragon's kingdom. He killed the Dragon, freed the lovely princess, married her and brought her back home with him. And the two of them lived happily ever after. They knew no woe, shed never a tear, and prospered the more from year to year.

Translated by Irina Zheleznova

Emelya and the Pike

In a certain village there once lived a peasant who had three sons, two of them clever young men, and the third, whose name was Emelya, a fool. The father had a long life and lived to a vast old age, and there came a day when he called his three sons to his side and said: "My dear children, I feel that I won't be with you long, so I leave you my house and what livestock I have to be divided equally amongst you, and also some money, a hundred rubles for each of you." Soon after that the father died, and the sons laid him to rest as it behooved them to and settled down to as happy a life as ever they had had before. One day Emelya's two clever brothers bethought them of going into town to trade and also to buy a number of things, and they said to Emelya: "Listen, fool, we are going into town to trade and taking your hundred rubles along with our own money. We'll go halves with you on the profits and we'll buy you a red caftan, a red hat and a pair of red boots. As for you, you're to stay at home, and if our wives and your sister-in-law ask you to do anything, you are to do it." And Emelya, who very much wanted to get the red caftan, red hat and red boots, said that he would do whatever was asked of him. The two brothers rode away, and the fool stayed at home with his sisters-in-law.

Some time passed, and one day, and a cold day it was, for it was winter, the sisters-in-law told him to fetch some water. But the fool, who was lying on top of the stove, said: "And what are you here for?" "What do you mean, fool?" the sisters-in-law shouted. "There's a terrible frost out, and it's a man has to fetch the water!" "I don't much feel like doing it," Emelya said. "Oh, you don't, do you!" they cried. "You'll want to eat, won't you, and how can we cook anything without water!" And they added: "Very well, then, we'll tell your brothers when they come back with the red caftan and the other things not to give you anything." Hearing this and being very eager to get the caftan, hat and boots, Emelya felt that there was nothing for it but to fetch the water, and so he climbed down from the stove and began to dress. He pulled on his felt boots and his coat, and, taking along two pails and an axe, went down to the river. He was there soon, for the river was not far from the village, and once there began cutting a hole in the ice. He made a great big one, and, scooping up two paifuls of water, set the pails down on the ice and himself stood there and stared at the water. And what did he see but a huge pike swimming in it. Now, foolish as he was, Emelya had the good sense to try and catch the pike, and so he started edging slowly up to the hole. He got very close to it, and then out shot his arm and there was the pike in his hands! He put it in his bosom and was about to go home when the pike said: "Wait, fool! What have you caught me for?" "What a question!" said Emelya. "I am going to take you home and ask my sister-in-law to cook you for our dinner." "Don't do it, fool! Let me go, and I'll make you rich." But Emelya would not believe the pike and clutched it fast. "Look here, fool," the pike said, "you must do as I ask. Put me back in the water, and I'll make your every wish come true." Hearing this and being very lazy, the fool was overjoyed. "If the pike makes my every wish come true, I'll never have to do any more work," said he to himself, "it'll all be done for me." And to the pike: "Very well, do as you promise, and I'll let you go." "Don't you worry, I'll keep my promise, just put me back in the water," the pike said. But the fool insisted that it do as it had said first.

Seeing that he was loath to let it go, the pike said: "If you want me to make your wish come true, you must tell me what your wish is." "I want my pails to go uphill all by themselves without spilling a drop of water," Emelya said. "It won't get spilled, never fear," said the pike. "You have only to say 'By the will of the pike do as I like' and then add 'Off you go up the hill, pails, all by yourselves!' and it will be done." "By the will of the pike do as I like!" Emelya said, and he added: "Off you go up the hill, pails, all by yourselves!" And lo and behold!—the pails turned and marched up the hill together with the yoke. Seeing that, Emelya was much surprised. "Will all be done as I wish in just this same way?" he asked. "Yes, if only you don't forget the words I told you to say," the pike replied. So Emelya slipped the pike back into the water and himself walked after his pails. Seeing him, the villagers stopped short and stood there marvelling. "What's this!" said they. "The pails are walking uphill all by themselves." But Emelya said not a

word and went after the pails into his house. The pails jumped up on a bench, and Emelya climbed up on the stove again.

Some time passed, and his sisters-in-law said to Emelya: "Why do you lie there, Emelya? Why don't you go and chop some wood?" "What are you here for?" Emelya said. "What do you mean!" they cried. "It's wintertime, and if you don't chop some wood you'll be the one to freeze." "I don't feel like chopping wood," Emelya said. "You don't, do you!" said they. "Well, freeze away, then. And don't forget that if you don't do as we say we'll tell your brothers not to give you the red caftan, hat and boots." Emelya, who very much wanted to get them, knew that the wood would have to be chopped, but as he was very lazy and loath to leave the stove top, he said half under his breath: "By the will of the pike do as I like! Go and chop some wood, axe, and you, logs, come into the hut and jump into the stove." And lo!—the axe whisked from under the bench and into the yard and began chopping the wood, and the logs marched into the hut and jumped into the stove all by themselves. The sisters-in-law stood there, their mouths open in surprise. And so it went. Every time Emelya was asked to chop some wood, the axe would do it for him.

Some time passed, and his sisters-in-law said to Emelya: "We have run out of firewood, Emelya. Go to the forest and cut some." "And what are you here for?" Emelya said. "What do you mean!" they said. "The forest is far away, and it's wintertime and much too cold for us to go there." "Well, I don't feel like going there either," Emelya said. "Oh, you don't, do you! Well, then, you'll just have to freeze. And when your brothers come home, we'll tell them not to give you anything: not the red caftan, nor the red hat and boots." And Emelya, who was very eager to get the caftan, hat and boots, felt that there was nothing for it but to go to the forest for the wood. So down he climbed from the stove and began to dress.

He put on his coat and felt boots, went out into the yard, dragged the sledge out of the shed, and, taking a length of rope and an axe, got into the sledge and told his sisters-in-law to open the gate. Seeing him in the sledge but with no horse harnessed to it, the sisters-in-law were quite taken aback. "What are you doing in the sledge, fool, why haven't you harnessed the horse!" they cried. "I don't need any horse, just you open the gate," Emelya told them. The sisters-in-law opened the gate, and he said half under his breath: "By the will of the pike do as I like! Off you go to the forest, sledge!" And no sooner were the words out of his mouth than the sledge drove out through the gate. Seeing it, the villagers stopped short and stood there marvelling, for it could not have moved any faster had two horses been harnessed to it!

Now, the road to the forest ran through a town, and as the fool did not know that he had to call out to warn the passers-by to get out of his way, he knocked down many. But though the townsfolk ran after him they could not catch him up.

He left the town behind him, and, coming to the forest, stopped the sledge, climbed out of it and said: "By the will of the pike do as I like! Cut some wood, axe, and you, logs, climb into the sledge one by one and bind yourselves together!" And no sooner were the words out of his mouth than the axe began cutting the wood, and the logs dropped into the sledge one by one and bound themselves together. When the sledge was full, he bade the axe make a cudgel for him, and when it had done so, he climbed on top of the load of wood and cried: "By the will of the pike do as I like! Off you go home, sledge, by yourself!" And the sledge rode off very fast indeed. It rode into the town where Emelya had knocked down many people, and there were the townsfolk ready and waiting for him. They seized him, pulled him out of the sledge and began beating him. And Emelya, seeing the plight he was in, said half under his breath: "By the will of the pike do as I like! Come, cudgel, give them a good walloping!" And the cudgel sprang up and laid to, right and left. The townsfolk took to their heels, and Emelya sped home in the sledge, and when the cudgel had beaten up all it could get at, it skipped down the road after him. And Emelya got home, stepped into the hut and climbed up on the stove again.

Emelya now became the talk of the town. And it wasn't so much because he had knocked down a great number of people, but because he had ridden in a sledge with no horse harnessed to it. At long last the king himself came to hear about him, and, being eager to see him, sent one of his officers and a number of soldiers to fetch him. The officer set out at once and soon came to the road Emelya had taken when he went to the forest for wood. This brought him to Emelya's village where he at once summoned the elder and told him that he had been sent there by the king to fetch Emelya and bring him to the palace. The elder showed him Emelya's house, and the officer came inside and looked about him. "Where is the fool?" he asked. And Emelya, lying on the stove top, said: "What do you want him for?" "Never mind. Put your things on quicky and I'll take you to the king's palace." "Why should I go there?" Emelya said. Hearing him speak so discourteously, the officer flew into a temper and slapped Emelya, and Emelya, who did not like it at all, said half under his breath: "By the will of the pike, do as I like! Come, cudgel, give them a good walloping!" And out the cudgel jumped and beat the officer and his men to within an inch of their lives. The officer fled, and as soon as he was back in town it was reported to the king what the fool had done. The king found it hard to believe that the fool could have

81

got the better of so many men, but he called one of the wisest men in the kingdom and sent him to fetch Emelya, by a ruse if need be. The man set out at once and as soon as he came to Emelya's village, sent for the elder and said: "The king bids me fetch the fool to the palace. Tell whoever he lives with that I wish to see them at once." The elder hastened to do as he was told and was soon back with Emelya's sisters-in-law: "He likes to be asked whatever one wants him to do again and again, gracious sir, and only then will he do it. There is nothing to be gained by being rough with him, but a kind word will go a long way." Bidding the two women not to tell Emelya that he had spoken to them, the man bought a bagful of raisins, prunes and figs and went to see him. He came into the house and up to the stove and asked Emelya why he was lying there. He then gave him the bag of sweets and begged him to go to the king's palace with him. "I'm all right where I am!" Emelya said. "It's nice and warm here." "Please, Emelya, come with me, you will like it in the palace," the man said. "I don't much feel like it!" said Emelya. "Now, Emelya, please do come!" said the man again. "The king will have a red caftan and hat made for you, and a pair of red boots too." Tempted, Emelya said: "Very well, then. Only you must go on alone and I will follow by and by." The man pressed him no more, and, stepping away from the stove, asked of the sisters-in-law in a whisper: "He is not trying to fool me, is he?" The sisters-in-law assured him that he was not, and the man left their house and set out for the palace.

As for Emelya, he lay on the stove a little while longer, and, saying with a sigh, "To go to see the king—what a bother!" added, "By the will of the pike do as I like! Off you go to the palace, stove!" And lo!—the hut began to creak, and off the stove whipped out of the hut and through the gate and so fast did it go that no one could have caught up with it. Emelya soon overtook the man who had been sent to fetch him, and they arrived at the palace together.

Seeing the fool waiting outside on top of the stove, the king came out of the palace with all his ministers to get a good look at him. "Why did you knock down so many people when you went to the forest for the wood?" he asked. "It wasn't my fault," Emelya said. "They shouldn't have got in my way." He glanced at the palace, and whom should he see standing at one of the windows looking out at him but the king's daughter. She was very beautiful, and Emelya said half under his breath: "By the will of the pike do as I like! Let that lovely maid fall in love with me!" And no sooner were the words out of his mouth than the king's daughter fell madly in love with him. "By the will of the pike do as I like! Off you go home, stove!" Emelya said. And off the stove made straight for Emelya's village. It whisked into his house and stood where it had stood before.

After that all went well for a time with Emelya, but not so well with the king, for his daughter was head over ears in love and she begged him to let her marry Emelya. This made the king very angry, but he did not know how he was to get Emelya back to the palace. He asked his ministers what they thought he should do, and they told him to send after him the officer who had failed to fetch him the first time. The officer was summoned, and the king said to him: "I sent you to fetch the fool once, my friend, and you failed to do it. So I am sending you after him again that you may prove your worth. If you succeed, I shall reward you; if you fail, I shall punish you." The officer set out at once for Emelya's village. And no sooner was he there than he sent for the elder and said: "Here is some money for you. Buy whatever you need to make a good meal. Tomorrow you are to invite Emelya to dinner in your house and to ply him with drink till he is so drunk that he will drop off to sleep."

Knowing that the officer had been sent by the king, the elder had no choice but to obey him. He bought everything he had been asked to and invited Emelya to dinner. Emelya said he would come, and, when told about it by the elder, the officer was well pleased. On the following day Emelya came to the elder's house and was plied with food and with so much drink that he was soon quite drunk and fell fast asleep. The officer at once bound him and had him put in a coach, and then, getting into the coach himself, drove straight to the palace with him. The ministers informed the king about his arrival, and the king at once ordered a large barrel bound with iron hoops to be brought. This was done, and seeing that everything was ready, the king had Emelya and the princess put in the barrel which was then tarred and sealed and cast in the sea.

The barrel bumped along on the waves, and many hours passed before Emelya woke. Seeing that there was darkness all about him and thinking himself to be quite alone, he called out in a loud voice: "Where am I?" "You are in a barrel, Emelya, and I am here with you," the princess said. "And who may you be?" Emelya asked. "I am the king's daughter." And she told him why she had been put in the barrel together with him and begged him to get them out of it. "I am all right where I am, it's nice and warm here," Emelya said. "Please, Emelya, take pity on me, don't make me cry," the princess said. "Surely you can get us out of this barrel." "I don't know about that," said Emelya. "I don't much feel like it." "Oh, please, you must not let me die, Emelya!" And Emelya, who was touched by her tears and entreaties, said: "Very well, I'll do as you ask." And he added half under his breath: "By the will of the pike, do as I like! Come, O sea, cast this barrel on to the shore, the closer to our own realm the better! And you, barrel, break open as soon as you are on dry land!"

And no sooner had he uttered these words than the sea rose in waves and the barrel was cast out on to dry land where it broke into pieces. Emelya and the princess walked along the shore and saw that they were on a beautiful island where grew many fruit trees. The princess liked it all very much, but said: "Where are we going to live, Emelya? There is nothing here, not even a hut." "Don't ask too much of me," Emelya said. "Please, Emelya, why don't you have a little house built? It might rain, and we don't want to get wet, do we!" said the princess, who knew that he could do anything if only he wanted to. "I don't feel like it," Emelya said. But she began pleading with him, and so touched was he that he knew he had to do as she asked. He walked a few steps away from her and said: "By the will of the pike do as I like! Let a palace more beautiful than the king's and filled with courtiers and servants arise on this island, and a crystal bridge too." And no sooner were the words out of his mouth than a huge palace and a crystal bridge rose up before him. Emelya and the princess came into the palace and found it to be richly decorated and teeming with people of all stations who waited to do Emelya's bidding. And Emelya, who saw that he alone of them all was both homely and a fool, was filled with a great urge to do something about it. "By the will of the pike do as I like!" said he. "I wish to become tall and handsome, and clever too, more handsome and clever than anyone!" And before the words were out of his mouth he became so handsome and so clever that everyone marvelled at the change in him.

After that Emelya sent a servant to the king to invite him and his ministers to his, Emelya's palace. The man crossed the crystal bridge and made his way to the king's palace, and when the king's ministers had ushered him into the king's presence, said: "My master has sent me to ask you to dine with him, Your Majesty." "Who is your master?" the king demanded. But the man, who had been told by Emelya to keep this a secret, said: "That is something no one knows. But when you have joined him he will tell you all you wish to know." The king, who was curious to find out who it was that had invited him to dine, told Emelya's servant that his master could expect him shortly, and as soon as the man had left, set out after him with his princes and ministers. And by the time Emelya learned that his invitation had been accepted, they were halfway across the crystal bridge.

The king rode up to Emelya's palace, and Emelya came out to meet him. He embraced him, led him into the palace, and, seating him and his princes and ministers at oaken tables covered with embroidered cloths, bade them taste of the many fine dishes and drink of the ale and mead. They ate and drank and made merry, and when they rose from their seats, Emelya asked of the king whether he knew who he was. But as Emelya was now so very handsome and dressed so very richly the king could not recognize him and said so. "Do you not recall, Your Majesty, how Emelya the Fool came to your palace on top of a stove and how you had him put in a tarred barrel together with you daughter and cast in the sea? Well, I am that very Emelya!" The king, frightened, stood there, not knowing what to say or do, and Emelya went after the princess and led her into his presence. The king could hardly believe his eyes. "I have done you much harm," said he, "and in order to atone for it am ready to give you my daughter in marriage." This made Emelya very happy. He thanked the king over and over again, and as everything had been put in readiness for the wedding it was celebrated the very same day in great style. And on the following day Emelya held a grand feast to which he invited all the ministers, while vats filled with wine and mead were set out by him for the ordinary folk. The merrymaking went on for many days, and when it was over, the king offered to give up both his crown and his throne to Emelya. But this Emelya refused, and the king went back to his own realm and left him in his palace where he lived for many long years without a care in the world.

Translated by Irina Zheleznova

The Fire-Bird
and Princess Vassilissa

In a certain kingdom, in a thrice-ten realm that lay far away, beyond the thrice-nine lands, there once lived a mighty king. The king had an archer who was as brave as he was strong, and the archer had a horse that was as strong as it was fleet of foot. One day the archer got on his horse and rode off to the forest to hunt.

He rode along a road, and a wide road it was, and he saw a fire-bird's feather lying there and flaming like fire! Said his horse to the archer: "Leave the feather where it is, for if you don't you will know a great misfortune." Now, this made the archer stop and think.

He was sorely tempted to take the feather, for if he presented it to the king, the king would surely reward him, and who is there that does not prize the favour of a king!

In the end, he decided to take it, and, picking it up, carried it away with him and presented it to the king. "Many thanks to you, Archer!" said the king. "But since you were able to fetch its feather, you must fetch me the fire-bird itself. If you don't it'll be out with my sword and off with your head!" The archer went back to his horse weeping bitterly. "Why do you weep, Master?" the horse asked. "The king has ordered me to fetch him the fire-bird." "I told you not to take the feather! Still, you must not fear or give way to despair. You are in no great trouble

86

now, there is worse to come! Just go to the king and ask him for a hundred bags of corn to be strewn over that field yonder." This the archer did, and the king had a hundred bags of corn strewn over the field.

At dawn on the following day the archer rode to the field. He unbridled his horse, let it roam there at will and himself hid behind a tree. All of a sudden the wind swept over the forest and sent it rustling, the sea rose in waves, and the fire-bird came flying to the field. Down it dropped and began pecking the corn, and the archer's horse ran up and stepped hard on one of its wings, pinning it to the ground. The archer then rushed out from behind the tree, and, binding the fire-bird with a rope, got on the horse with it and rode at a gallop for the palace. He presented the fire-bird to the king, who was greatly pleased, thanked the archer for serving him so well, promoted him and at once set him another task. "You were able to fetch the fire-bird, so you should be able to fetch me the maid I wish to marry, Princess Vassilissa. She lives at the very end of the earth, where the bright sun rises, and it is her I want and none other. If you bring her to me, I will shower you with gold and silver, but if you don't, it'll be out with my sword and off with your head!"

The archer went back to his horse weeping bitterly. "Why do you weep, Master?" the horse asked. "The king bids me fetch him Princess Vassilissa." "Do not weep or be sad. You are in no great trouble, there is worse to come! Go to the king and ask him for a gold-topped tent and for food and drink for you to take with you on your journey." The king gave him food and drink and a tent with a top of gold, and the archer got on his horse and set off on his way. Beyond thrice-nine lands he travelled, and whether a short or a long time passed nobody knows, but he came at last to the end of the earth, where the bright sun rises from the blue sea. And there on the sea, in a silver boat that she pushed with a paddle of gold, was Princess Vassilissa herself. The archer unbridled his horse and let it roam at will in the green meadow and pick at the fresh grass, and then he set up the gold-topped tent, put foods and drinks on a table, and sat down to eat and drink while he waited for Princess Vassilissa.

And Princess Vassilissa saw the gold top gleaming in the sunlight, paddled to shore, and, stepping out of the boat, stood there looking admiringly at the tent. "Good morrow to you, Princess Vassilissa!" the archer said. "Pray come in and share of my board and taste of the wines I brought from far-off lands." Princess Vassilissa came into the tent and she and the archer ate and drank and made merry. A whole glass of wine did she drink and was so overcome that she fell fast asleep. The archer called his horse, and when it came running, folded the tent with the top of gold, picked up Princess Vassilissa, mounted the horse with her in his arms, and set off home. As fast as an arrow he flew and was soon in the palace.

The king was overjoyed at the sight of Princess Vassilissa. He thanked the archer for having served him so well and gave him a still higher rank. But when Princess Vassilissa awoke and learnt that she was far, far away from the blue sea, she began sobbing and weeping and her face turned dark with grief. And though the king pleaded with her not to be sad, there was nothing he could do. He begged her to marry him, but she said: "Let him who brought me here go to my realm at the end of the earth and fetch my wedding dress which lies under a large rock in the middle of the sea. I will not marry without it!" The king sent for the archer. "Go at once to the end of the earth where the bright sun rises. In the middle of the sea you will find a large rock and under it Princess Vassilissa's wedding dress. Bring the dress here, for I wish to wed without delay! If you bring it, I shall reward you richly, more so than ever before, but if you don't, it'll be out with my sword and off with your head!" Back went the archer to his horse weeping bitterly. "I will not escape death this time!" said he to himself. "Why do you weep, Master?" the horse asked. "The king bids me fetch him Princess Vassilissa's wedding dress from the bottom of the sea." "Didn't I tell you not to take the fire-bird's feather? But never fear, you are in no great trouble, there is worse to come! Get on my back and let us go to the blue sea."

Whether a short or a long time passed nobody knows, but the archer came to the end of the earth and stopped on the shore of the blue sea. A huge lobster came crawling over the sand toward him, and the horse saw it and stepped on its tail with its hoof. Said the lobster: "Spare me, Horse, do not let me die! I will do whatever you ask." And the horse said in reply: "There is a great rock lying on the bottom of the sea and hidden under it is Princess Vassilissa's wedding dress. Fetch the dress for me!"

The lobster gave a great roar that carried over the whole of the sea, the sea rose in waves, and lobsters, big and small, came crawling to the shore from all sides. And so many were they that there was no counting them! The lobster who had called them and who was their elder bade them fetch the dress, and they plunged into the sea and came back with it before an hour had passed.

The archer brought the dress to the king, but Princess Vassilissa was as stubborn as ever and said that she would not marry him until he had made the archer take a dip in boiling water. The king at once ordered an iron cauldron to be filled with water, the water to be heated, and as soon as it came to the boil, the archer to be thrown in it. Everything was soon ready, the water began to seethe and to boil, sprays of it flying to all sides, and the archer was led in. "Poor, unhappy man that I am!" thought he. "What made me take the fire-bird's feather? Why didn't I listen to my horse?" And recalling the horse, he said to the king: "O great king, my ruler, allow me to bid my horse goodbye before I die!" "Very well," said the king. The archer went to see the horse, and the tears poured from his eyes. "Why do you weep, Master?" the horse asked. "The king bids me dip myself in boiling water." "Fear nothing and do not weep, you will not die!" said the horse, and he cast a spell over the archer that he might not get scalded by the boiling water. The archer left the stall, and the king's servants seized him and threw him into the cauldron. He took a dip and another and jumped out of the cauldron, and lo!—so handsome had he become as neither pen can write nor tongue tell! Seeing this, the king took it into his head to take a dip himself. He jumped into the cauldron and was boiled alive! And after he was buried the archer was chosen to rule the realm in his stead. He married Princess Vassilissa and they lived together for many long years and were as happy as happy can be.

Translated by Irina Zheleznova

The Horse, the Table-Cloth and the Horn

There was once an old woman whose son was a fool. One day the fool found three peas. He went out of the village and planted them. When the shoots came up, he kept watch over them. One day he came to the spot and saw a crane pecking at the plants. The fool crept up and caught the crane. "Aha!" he said. "I'm going to kill you." But the crane said to him: "Please don't kill me! I'll give you a present." "Very well," agreed the fool. The crane gave him a horse, saying: "If you want some money say 'Go!' to this horse, and when you have enough say 'Stop!'"

The fool took the horse, mounted it and said "Go!" The horse turned into a pile of silver. The fool laughed gleefully and then said "Stop!" And the silver turned back into a horse. The fool bade farewell to the crane and led the horse home, taking it through the yard, right into the house to his mother. He gave her strict instructions: "Don't say 'Go!' Only say 'Stop!' mother." And went to keep watch over his peas. His mother puzzled for a long time: "Why did he tell me those words? What if I do say 'Go!' instead?" And she said it. The horse turned into a pile of silver. The old woman's eyes lit up. She hurriedly scooped the money into her chest and when she had enough said "Stop!"

Meanwhile the fool again found the crane eating his peas, caught it and threatened to kill it. But the crane said: "Please don't kill me. I'll give you a present." And it gave him a table-cloth. "When you are hungry say 'Unfold!' and when you have eaten your fill say 'Fold up!'" The fool immediately tried it out.

"Unfold!" he said, and the table-cloth unfolded. He ate and drank his fill and ordered "Fold up!" And the table-cloth folded itself up. He took it home. "Now listen, mother. Don't say 'Unfold!' to the table-cloth, only say 'Fold up!'" Then the fool went to keep watch over his peas again. His mother did the same with the table-cloth as with the horse. She said "Unfold!" and proceeded to eat and drink everything on the cloth, then ordered "Fold up!" and the table-cloth folded itself up.

On the pea patch the fool again caught the crane, who presented him with a horn and called out as it flew up into the air: "Say 'Out of the horn!'" To his great misfortune the fool did as the crane bade him, and two strapping young men with cudgels leapt out of the horn and beat him until he fell to the ground. Then the crane called out from above "Into the horn!" and the two young men disappeared. The fool went home to his mother and said: "Don't say 'Out of the horn!' Say 'Into the horn!' instead, mother." As soon as the fool had gone round to the neighbours, his mother latched the door and said "Out of the horn!" Whereupon the two strapping young men with cudgels leapt out and began to beat the old woman, who yelled the house down. The fool heard her screams and ran home as fast as his legs could carry him. Seeing that the door was latched, he shouted, "Into the horn! Into the horn!" When the old woman had recovered from her drubbing, she opened the door and let the fool in. "Serves you right, mother!" she said. "I told you not to say that."

The fool decided to give a feast and invited all the lords and ladies. When they had arrived and sat down, he led the horse into the house and said: "Go, trusty steed!" The horse turned into a pile of silver. The guests were astounded and began to snatch up the silver and hide it in their pockets. Then the fool said "Stop!" and the horse reappeared, without its tail. The fool saw it was time to feed the guests, so he got out the table-cloth and said: "Unfold!" The table-cloth unfolded and all manner of food and drink appeared on it. The guests began to eat, drink and make merry. When they had eaten their fill, the fool said: "Fold up!" And the table-cloth folded up. The guests began to yawn and scoff: "Show us something else, fool." "With pleasure," said the fool. "I've got just the thing for you!" And he brought out the horn. The guests shouted: "Out of the horn!" Then the two strapipng young men leapt out and began to beat them with all their might until the guests gave back the money they had stolen and ran off as fast as their legs would carry them. And the fool and his mother lived happily ever after with the horse, the table-cloth and the horn.

Translated by Kathleen Cook

Go I Know Not Where, Bring I Know Not What

Tarabanov the soldier went off to seek his fortune. He walked on and on for a week, then another, then a third, and come twelve-month he crossed the thrice-nine land, reached the thrice-ten kingdom and entered a dense forest with nothing but trees and sky. By and by he saw an open glade and in the glade a great palace. He gazed at the palace and marvelled at such riches, the like of which had ne'er been known before, save in the fairy tales of yore. Walking round the palace, he saw that there was neither gate nor door, nor entrance of any kind. So he picked up a long pole lying on the ground, stood it against a balcony, took his courage in both hands and shinned up it; then he climbed onto the balcony, opened the glass doors and strolled round the chambers. There was not a soul to be seen. The place was deserted.

The soldier entered the grand hall. There he saw a round table with twelve dishes of all sorts of food and twelve carafes of sweet wine. Feeling hungry, he took a morsel from each dish and poured a glassful from each carafe. Having eaten and drunk his fill, he climbed onto the stove-bed, made a pillow of his knapsack and lay down to rest. Before he had time to doze off, twelve swans flew in through the window, struck the floor and turned into twelve beautiful maidens, each one fairer than the last. They laid their wings on the stove, sat down at the table and began to eat and drink, each from her own dish and her own carafe. "There is something wrong, sisters," said one of them. "Someone has drunk of our wine and eaten of our food." "Be quiet, sister! You tnink you're so clever!" The soldier had seen where they put their wings. He got up quietly, took the pair belonging to the clever maiden and hid them.

The beautiful maidens dined, left the table and hurried to the stove to put on their wings. There was one pair missing. "Oh, sisters, my wings have gone!" "Serves you right for being so clever!" The eleven maidens struck the floor, turned back into white swans and flew out of the window. The twefth, left all alone, began to weep bitterly. The soldier climbed down from the stove. The maid saw him and implored him to give back her wings. "Beg and weep as much as you like, I'll never give back your wings. So you'd best consent to be my wife and live together with me." Then they came to an understanding and hugged and kissed each other.

The fair maiden took her betrothed down into the cellars, opened a large chest bound with iron and said: "Take as much gold as you can carry, so we have enough to set up house and live on for the rest of our days." The soldier filled his pockets with gold, pulled the well-worn shirts out of his knapsack and stuffed it with gold too. Then they set off together on their long journey.

By and by they came to the fair capital city, rented some chambers and set up house. One day the soldier's wife said to him: "Take this hundred rubles. Go to the shop and spend it all on silk for me." The soldier went off. On the way he passed a tavern. "Surely I could spend ten kopecks of this hundred rubles on a drink?" he thought. So in he went, drank half a bottle of liquor, paid his ten kopecks and set off to buy the silk. He got a big roll of silk, took it home and gave it to his wife. "How much was this?" she asked. "A hundred rubles." "No, it wasn't. You paid a hundred rubles less ten kopecks for it. What did you do with the ten kopecks? Had a drink in the tavern, I'll bet!" "She's a clever one and no mistake," thought the soldier. "No fooling her!" From the silk the soldier's wife sewed three beautful carpets and sent her husband to sell them. A rich merchant paid three thousand for each of them, waited until a big feast day and gave the carpets to the king himself as a present. "What dexterous hands sewed these!" exclaimed the king in amazement. "They are the work of a common soldier's wife, Sire," replied the merchant. "Surely not! Where does she live? I will visit her myself."

The very next day the king visited the soldier's wife to order some new work from her. When he set eyes upon her beauty, he fell head over heels in love with her. He returned to the palace and began scheming to get the wife away from her husband. Summoning his favourite general, he said: "Think of an excuse to get a soldier out of the way. I will reward you with high rank, land and gold." "Give him a difficult task, Your Majesty. Send him to the ends of the earth to bring back Saura the Servant. Saura the Servant will live in your pocket and do whatever you tell him as quick as lightning!"

95

The king sent for the soldier and began rebuking him as soon as he was brought to the palace: "Foolish fellow! Fancy boasting in all the taverns that getting hold of Saura the Servant is as easy as pie. Why didn't you come to me first, instead of keeping quiet. You know my doors are closed to no one." "I would never dream of boasting such a thing, Your Majesty!" "Now then, my man, don't go back on your word! You must go to the ends of the earth and bring me back Saura the Servant. If you do not, I'll have you put to death!" The soldier went home to his wife and told her the bad tidings. She took out a ring and handed it to him, saying: "Follow this ring wherever it leads you and fear nothing!" Then she gave him some parting words of wisdom and sent him on his way.

The ring rolled along until it reached a little wooden house, then jumped onto the porch, through the door and under the stove. The soldier followed it inside, crawled under the stove and waited. Suddenly a thumb-sized mannikin with a long, long beard came in and called out: "Hey, Saura! Where's my dinner?" Quick as lightning a roasted ox with a knife in its loin and garlic in its groin appeared in front of him, together with a forty-gallon barrel of good beer. The thumb-sized mannikin with the long, long beard sat down by the ox, pulled out the knife and proceeded to carve the meat, dip it in the garlic, eat it and sing its praises. He picked the ox clean, downed the whole barrel of beer and said: "Thank you, Saura! Your food is good. I shall come again in three years' time." Then he took his leave and went away.

The soldier climbed out from under the stove, plucked up his courage and shouted: "Hey, Saura! Are you there?" "Yes, soldier!" "Then give me some dinner too." Saura brought him a roast ox and a forty-gallon barrel of beer. "That's far too much for me, Saura," the soldier exclaimed. "I couldn't eat and drink all that in a twelve-month." He had a few slices and drank about a bottle, thanked Saura for the meal and asked: "How would you like to serve me, Saura?" "Willingly, sir, if you will take me. My old man is such a glutton that I wear myself out trying to satisfy his appetite." "Let's go then. Climb into my pocket." "I'm there already, sir."

Tarabanov went out of the house. Off rolled the ring to show them the way and, by and by, it led the soldier home. He straightway went to the palace, called Saura out and left him to serve the king. The king again summoned his general. "You said Tarabanov would perish and never fetch Saura, but he has returned hale and hearty with Saura in his pocket!" "Then we must find out how your late father is faring there." Without further ado the king dispatched a messenger to summon Tarabanov the soldier to the palace. The messenger rode there post-haste: "Hey, soldier-boy, get dressed. The king wants you."

The soldier polished the buttons on his greatcoat, got dressed, sat down beside the messenger and rode to the palace. When he appeared before the king, the king said to him: "Listen, foolish fellow! Why did you go boasting in all the taverns that you could visit the after-world and find out how my late father is faring, without a word to me?" "For pity's sake, Your Majesty! I would never dream of boasting such a thing. I know of no way to visit the after-world save by dying, so help me!" "Well, be that as it may, you must go and find out about my father, or my sword will have your head from your shoulders!" Sad at heart, Tarabanov returned home, his curly head drooping between his powerful shoulders. "Why so downcast, dear heart?" asked his wife. "Tell me all." So he told her the whole story. "Never mind, do not worry. Just go to bed. Morning is wiser than evening."

The next morning, as soon as the soldier awoke, his wife said: "Go to the king and ask him to let you take as your companion the general who keeps thinking up tasks for you." Tarabanov dressed, went to the king and asked: "Let me take the general to keep me company, Your Majesty. Let him witness that I have indeed visited the after-world and found out about your revered parent without any trickery." "Very well, my man! Go home and prepare for the journey. I will send him to you." Tarabanov went home and prepared for the journey. Meanwlile the king summoned the general. "You must go with the soldier too," he said. "He is not to be trusted alone." The general was scared out of his wits, but there was nothing for it. A king's word is not to be disobeyed. So off he went unwillingly to the soldier's home.

Tarabanov filled his knapsack with rusks and his flask with water, bade farewell to his wife, took the ring from her and said to the general: "Let us be on our way." They went into the yard. A carriage and four was standing by the porch. "Who's that for?" asked the soldier. "What do you mean? For us, of course." "No, Your Excellency. We have no need of a carriage. The way to the after-world is on foot." The ring rolled along, followed by the soldier, with the general puffing and panting behind. It was a long journey. When the soldier felt hungry he took a rusk from his knapsack, soaked it in the water and munched it, while his companion watched with his mouth watering. If the soldier treated him to a rusk, all well and good, but if not he would go hungry.

Time went by, how much who can say? The tale is told ere the deed is done. By and by they came to a dense forest and went down into a deep ravine. Here the ring stopped. The soldier and the general sat down on the ground and began to eat rusks. Before they had finished, they saw the old king pulling a cart piled high with firewood, while two devils urged him on with cudgels, one on his right and the other on his left. "Look, Your Excellency! Isn't that the old king?" "Yes, His Majesty is carting firewood!" "Hey, there, master devils!" shouted the soldier. "Let me have that old fellow for a moment. There's something I must ask him." "We haven't got all day. Who'll cart the firewood while you're talking to him? Not us!" "Why should you! Here, take this new man in his place."

The devils quickly unharnessed the old king from the cart, put the general in his place, and gave him a taste of their cudgels. Off the general trotted, puffing and panting. Then the soldier asked the old king how he was faring in the after-world. "Badly, soldier, badly! Take greetings to my son and bid him have prayers said for my soul, then perhaps the Lord will take mercy on me and free me from eternal torment. And charge him strictly in my name not to offend the common folk or the soldiery, or the good Lord will punish him!" "He may not believe my word. Give me some token." "Take this key! When he sees it, he will believe all." They had barely finished their conversation, when the devils came back. The soldier bade farewell to the old king, collected the general and set off home with him.

They reached their kingdom and went straight to the palace. "Your Majesty," said the soldier to the king. "I have seen your late revered parent, and he is faring badly in the after-world. He sends you greetings and bids you have prayers said for his soul so that the good Lord may free him from eternal torment. And he bade me charge you strictly not to offend the common folk or the soldiery! For the Lord punishes that most severly." "But did you in truth go to the after-world and see my father?" Then the general said: "My back still bears the marks where the devils beat me with their cudgels." But the soldier handed over the key. "Ah!" exclaimed the king, "this is the secret cabinet key that they forgot to remove from my father's pocket when they buried him!" Then the king no longer doubted that the soldier was telling the truth. He made him general and stopped coveting his fair wife.

Translated by Kathleen Cook

The King of the Sea
and Vassilissa the Wise

Beyond the thrice-nine lands, in the thrice-ten kingdom there once lived a king and queen who had no children. One day the king went travelling to distant lands and was away from home for a long time, and in his absence the queen gave birth to a son whom she named Prince Ivan. Of this the king knew nothing. He was on his way back to his own realm and was not far from it, when, the day being very, very hot, he felt so thirsty that he would have given anything for a drink of water! He looked about him, and, seeing a large lake ahead, rode up to it, got off his horse, lay down on the ground on his belly and began taking great gulps of the icy lake water. He drank and he drank and did not know there was anything to fear when all of a sudden someone clutched him by the beard! "Let go of my beard!" he cried. "No, I won't! How dare you drink this water without my permission?" said the King of the Sea, for it was he who was clutching the beard. "Take any ransom you want of me, only let me go!" "Promise to give me that which you have in your house but do not know about." The king thought it over, and, being quite sure that there was nothing in his house he did not know about, agreed. He felt his beard, saw that no one was clutching it any more, and, getting to his feet, mounted his horse and rode away.

He came home, and there was the queen, as happy as could be, welcoming him back! She was holding the baby in her arms, and when the king learnt that he had a son, he burst into tears. He told the queen about the King of the Sea, and she wept with him, but what could they do! And as for Prince Ivan, he grew and grew, not by the day but by the hour, as fat as dough with yeast added to it, and before long was quite grown. "I can't keep him with me forever, I'm afraid," thought the king. "The day will come when I'll have to give him up to the King of the Sea, there's no avoiding it!" He took Prince Ivan by the hand and led him to the lake. "Look for my ring, I dropped it here somewhere the other day," said he, and, leaving Prince Ivan all by himself, turned his way homewards.

Prince Ivan began looking for the ring, and as he walked along the shore, he met an old woman coming toward him. "Where are you going, Prince Ivan?" she asked. "Leave me alone, you old witch, I have trouble enough as it is!" Prince Ivan said. "Oh, all right, then, and may God be with you!" And the old woman left him and turned off the road. But Prince Ivan regretted having behaved so badly. "Now, why was I so rude to the old woman?" he asked himself. "I'd better go after her and get her to come back. Old people are wise; she may be able to tell me something that will be of help to me." And he called to the old woman, begging her to forgive him for his foolish words and come back. "It was because I was troubled that I was so rude," said he. "My father told me to look for his ring, but though I have looked and looked I cannot find it anywhere." "It isn't because of the ring that your father brought you here," the old woman said, "but because he promised the King of the Sea that you would be his. The King of the Sea will soon appear and take you away with him to his underwater kingdom."

Prince Ivan burst into tears. "Do not grieve, Prince Ivan, luck will yet come your way," said the old woman. "Only you must listen to me. Hide behind that currant bush there and keep very quiet. By and by twelve doves, fair maids all, will come flying here, and a thirteenth will follow them. They will bathe and splash about in the water, and while they are at it, you must carry off the thirteenth maid's shift and not give it back to her till she gives you her ring. If you fail to do this, you are lost, for the King of the Sea has a high fence a full ten miles long round his palace, with a human head crowning every paling. One paling only has no head on it, so beware lest it be crowned with yours!" Prince Ivan thanked the old woman and hid behind the currant bush.

All of a sudden twelve doves came flying to the lake shore. They struck the ground and turned into maids so fair as pen cannot write or tongue tell! They flung off their gown and rushed into the water, and they played and splashed about there merrily. Then the thirteenth dove came flying up. It struck the ground and turned into a maid, and of them all, fair as they were, she was the fairest! She took off her gown and shift and stepped into the water, and Prince Ivan could not take his eyes from her so smitten was he, but then, recalling what the old woman had told him, he crept out from behind the bush and carried off the shift.

The maid came out of the water and looked about for her shift. It was not there, and though she and her sisters searched and searched for it, they could not find it. "Do not search for it any longer but fly home!" said the maid to her sisters. "It's my fault that I did not keep an eye on it and I must be the one to answer for it." And the twelve maids, her sisters, struck the ground, and, turning into doves, flapped their wings and flew away. The maid was left alone, and she looked all around her and said: "You, whoever you are, who have my shift, come out and show yourself! If you are old, you shall be as my own father to me; if you are in your middle years, you shall be as a brother to me; if you are of an age with me, you shall be my own dear love!" And she no sooner uttered the last word than Prince Ivan appeared before her. She gave him her gold ring and said: "Ah, Prince Ivan, why did you not come here sooner? The King of the Sea is sorely vexed with you. Yonder lies the road that leads to his underwater kingdom. Follow it without fear and you will find me at the end of it! For I am Vassilissa the Wise, daughter of the King of the Sea." Vassilissa the Wise turned into a dove and flew away, and Prince Ivan set out for the underwater kingdom which, when he got there, he found to be, what with the sun shining overhead and green fields, meadows and groves everywhere, very much like any kingdom on earth. He came into the presence of the King of the Sea, and the King of the Sea roared at the top of his voice: "What made you tarry so long? Why did you not come here sooner? I shall punish you for it by setting you a task! I have a waste plot of land thirty miles long and thirty wide, which is all ditches, gullies and sharp stones. Now, I want this to be made as smooth as the palm of a man's hand and sown with rye, and the rye to be high enough by tomorrow morning for a jackdaw to hide in. And if you do not do it, I'll have your head cut off!"

Prince Ivan left the King of the Sea, and the tears poured from his eyes. And Vassilissa the Wise, sitting at the window of her chamber, saw him and said: "Good morrow, Prince Ivan! Why do you weep?" "How can I help it!" said Prince Ivan. "The King of the Sea bids me level his waste plot of land which is all ditches, gullies and sharp stones, to sow it with rye and to have the rye grow high enough by morning for a jackdaw to hide in." "That is no great misfortune, there is worse to come. Go to bed and to sleep with God's help. Night is the mother of wisdom, and all will be done for you!" Prince Ivan went to bed, and Vassilissa the Wise stepped out on the porch and called in a loud voice: "Come, my faithful servants, fill in the ditches and gullies, bear off the sharp stones, plough up the plot and sow it with rye, and have it all done by tomorrow morning!"

Prince Ivan woke with the dawn, he looked about him, and lo!—everything had been done: not a ditch or a gully was there, the ground had all been levelled, the plot sown with rye, and the rye had grown high enough for a jackdaw to hide in. He went and told the King of the Sea about it, and the King of the Sea said: "Thank you for doing as I bade. And now here is another task for you. I have three hundred stacks of wheat, with three hundred sheaves in each, and you are to thresh it all for me to the last grain and yet leave every single one of the sheaves and stacks whole, and if this is not done by morning, I'll have your head cut off!" "I will do as you bid, Your Majesty!" said Prince Ivan, and as he walked out of the palace and across the courtyard the tears poured from his eyes. "Why do you weep?" Vassilissa the Wise asked him. "How can I help it! The King of the Sea

bids me thresh all of his wheat in the space of one night, and I am not to lose a single grain and keep all of the stacks and sheaves whole." "That is no great misfortune, there is worse to come! Go to bed and to sleep, and may God be with you. Night is the mother of wisdom, remember!"

Prince Ivan went to bed, and Vassilissa the Wise stepped out on to the porch and called in a loud voice: "Come, ants, crawl here, all of you, as many as there are in the world, pick out the grains from my father's stacks of wheat and do not leave a single grain behind!" Morning came, and the King of the Sea summoned Prince Ivan. "Have you done as I bade?" he asked. "I have, Your Majesty!" "Come along, then, I wish to see it for myself." They came to the threshing floor, and there were all the stacks whole and of a piece; they came to the granary, and it was filled to the top with grain. "Thank you, my lad!" said the King of the Sea. "Just build me a church out of wax and have it ready by morning, and I will ask you to do nothing more." Off went Prince Ivan, and as he crossed the courtyard the tears poured from his eyes. "Why do you weep?" Vassilissa the Wise, sitting at the window of her chamber high up in the palace, asked him. "How can I help it! The King of the Sea bids me build him a church out of wax in the space of one night." "That is no great misfortune, there is worse to come. Go to bed and to sleep; night is the mother of wisdom, remember!"

Prince Ivan went to bed, and Vassilissa the Wise stepped out on to the porch and called in a loud voice: "Come, bees, all of you, from all over the world, fly here and build a church of wax in the space of one night!"

Morning came, Prince Ivan rose, and there stood the church before him, made of the purest wax! He went and told the King of the Sea about it, and the King of the Sea said: "I thank you, Prince Ivan! Many are the servants I have had, but not one of them pleased me as you have. Be my heir and the defender of my realm! And you can take to wife whichever one you choose of my thirteen daughters." Prince Ivan chose Vassilissa the Wise, they were at once married, there was great joy in the palace, and a feast was held which went on for three days.

Whether a short or a long time passed nobody knows, but Prince Ivan missed his parents and badly wanted to go back to Russ. "Why so sad, Prince Ivan?" Vassilissa the Wise asked him. "Ah, now there is indeed a great misfortune ahead! For if we leave this realm, many men will be sent after us to try to bring us back, and the King of the Sea will be greatly angered and have us put to death. But we may yet outwit them all!" And she went and sprayed three of the corners of their sleeping chamber with water, and, leaving it and locking the door behind her, rode away together with Prince Ivan.

Early on the following morning the servants of the King of the Sea came to rouse the young couple and summon them into the King's presence, and they knocked at the door of their chamber and called: "Wake up! Wake up! The King wishes to see you." "It's much too early, come a little later!" the drops of water called back in Vassilissa's own voice. The servants went away, but they came back again in an hour or so and knocked at the door again. "Time to get up!" they called. "Wait a little while, we have to get dressed!" the drops of water called back. Another hour passed, and the servants came back for the thrid time. "The King of the Sea is vexed with you, you must not dawdle any longer!" they called. "We'll be with him in a moment!" the drops of water called back. The servants waited a while longer and began knocking at the door again, but there was no reply, so they broke down the door, and lo!—the chamber was empty. They told the King that the young couple had run away, and he flew into a temper and sent many men after them to bring them back.

By then Vassilissa the Wise and Prince Ivan had left the palace far behind them. They galloped on their fleet-footed steeds and never so much as stopped for a rest. "Come, Prince Ivan, put your ear to the ground and see if you can hear anything," said Vassilissa the Wise. Prince Ivan jumped down from his horse's back and put his ear to the ground. "I can hear men calling and hooves pounding," he said. "That means the King's men are after us!" said Vassilissa the Wise, and she at once turned the horses into a green meadow, Prince Ivan into a shepherd and herself into a sheep.

The King's men were soon upon them. "Tell us, shepherds," they called, "have you seen a youth and a maid riding past here?" "No, kind folk, I have not," replied Prince Ivan. "I have been grazing sheep here for forty years, and never has a bird flown past or a beast run by in all that time." The King's men went back to the palace. "We have not seen anyone on the way, Your Majesty, save a shepherd and a sheep," said they. "And you should have seized them, for they were the ones I sent you after!" roared the King, and he sent more of his men after the runaways. Prince Ivan and Vassilissa the Wise were far away by then, and Vassilissa the Wise said: "Come, Prince Ivan, put your ear to the ground and see if you can hear anything." Prince Ivan jumped down from his hourse's back and put his ear to the ground. "I can hear men calling and hooves pounding," said he. "The King's men are coming after us!" said Vassilissa the Wise, and she turned herself into a church, Prince Ivan into a priest and the horses into trees.

The King's men were soon upon them. "Tell us, Father, have you seen a shepherd passing by here with a flock of sheep?" they called. "No, kind folk, I have not," said Prince Ivan. "I have been with this church for forty years, but never has a bird flown past or a beast run by in all that time." The men went back to the palace. "We have seen no shepherd or sheep on the way, Your Majesty," said they. "We only saw a church and a priest standing by it." "Why didn't you pull down the church and seize the priest? They were the ones I sent you after!" roared the King, and he got on his horse and, followed by his men, set out after the runaways himself.

By then Prince Ivan and Vassilissa the Wise were far away. "Come, Prince Ivan, put your ear to the ground and see if you can hear anything," Vassilissa the Wise said. Prince Ivan climbed off his horse's back and put his ear to the ground.

"I can hear men calling and hooves pounding more loudly than ever," said he. "That is the King himself coming after us with his men!" Vassilissa the Wise cried, and she turned the horses into a lake, Prince Ivan into a drake and herself took the shape of a duck. The King of the Sea came galloping up to the lake, and he at once guessed who the duck and the drake were. He struck the ground, turned into an eagle and swooped down upon them from above, but though he did this again and again the drake and the duck were too quick for him and dived into the water before he could get at them! By and by, seeing that he could do nothing, he gave up and galloped away, back to his underwater kingdom. And Vassilissa the Wise and Prince Ivan waited awhile and then set off for Russ.

Whether a short or a long time passed nobody knows, but by and by they came to Russ. "Wait for me in this wood," said Prince Ivan to Vassilissa the Wise, "and I'll go on ahead and show myself to my mother and father." "You will forget me, Prince Ivan!" "I won't." "You will, I know it! But you must try and remember me when you see two doves beating against a window pane." Prince Ivan came into the palace, and, seeing him, his parents threw their arms around him and held him close, and in his joy Prince Ivan forgot all about Vassilissa the Wise. He lived with his mother and father for a day and another day, and on the third day bethought him of marrying a princess he had met in the palace.

And Vassilissa the Wise went into town and took up service with a priest's widow who made wafers for a living. They began making wafers, and she took two pieces of dough, fashioned two doves out of them and put them in the oven. "Do you know what will happen to these doves, mistress?" asked she. "No, for what can happen to them? We'll eat them, that's all." "Do you really think so?" And Vassilissa the Wise opened the oven and then the window, and lo!—the doves started up and flew straight to the palace. They began beating at the windows there, and try as the King's servants might they could not chase them away. Then it was that Prince Ivan remembered Vassilissa the Wise and sent envoys to all corners of the realm to try and find her. She was soon found and brought to the palace, and he took her snow-white hands in his, kissed her on her sugar-sweet lips and led her to his mother and father. And from that day on all the four of them knew no woe, shed never a tear, and prospered the more from year to year.

Translated by Irina Zheleznova

Fenist the Falcon

There once lived an old man who had three daughters. The two elder daughters thought of nothing but of dressing themselves up in fancy clothes, but the youngest cared little for such things and liked to keep house and tend the garden far more. One day the old man prepared to go to market and he asked his daughters what they wanted him to buy for them. The eldest daughter told him that she would like a length of silk for a dress, and so did the middle daughter, but when he turned to the youngest daughter, she said: "Buy me a feather of Fenist the Falcon, Father." The father bade his daughters goodbye and away he rode. He brought his two elder daughters what they had asked for, but he could not find Fenist the Falcon's feather anywhere. He came back home, and, oh, how pleased the two elder daughters were with the lengths of silk! But for the youngest daughter there was nothing. "I could not find Fenist the Falcon's feather anywhere," the father told her. "Well, it can't be helped!" she said. "Perhaps you will have better luck next time." The two elder sisters sat down and began making dresses for themselves, and they laughed at their younger sister, but she kept very quiet and paid them no heed.

By and by the father prepared to go to market again. "Well, daughters, what would you like me to buy for you this time?" he asked. The elder daughter told him that she would like a shawl, and so did the middle daughter, but the youngest daughter said: "Buy me a feather of Fenist the Falcon, Father." Off the father rode, he bought the two shawls, but he never so much as laid eyes on the feather.

He came back home and said to his youngest daughter: "Ah, child, I could not find a feather of Fenist the Falcon for you this time, either." "Never mind, Father, perhaps you will have better luck next time!" said she.

By and by the father prepared to go to market for the third time. "Come, daughters, what would you like me to buy for you?" he asked them. The eldest daughter asked for a pair of earrings, and so did the middle daughter, but the youngest daughter said as she had before: "Buy me a feather of Fenist the Falcon, Father." The father bought two pairs of gold earrings, but though he looked everywhere no feather could he find. Saddened, he set out for home, but just as he had left the town gate behind him, he met an old man bearing a little box in his hands. "What have you there, old man?" he asked. "A feather of Fenist the Falcon." "How much do you want for it?" "A thousand pieces of gold." The father paid the money and drove home with the box. His daughters met him at the door. "Well, my dear," said he, turning to the youngest daughter, "I have brought what you asked for at last. Here, take it!" The youngest daughter all but danced with joy. She took the box and kissed it and pressed it to her heart.

After supper they all went off to bed, and she ran to her chamber and opened the box, and lo!—out of it flew Fenist the Falcon's feather. If lighted on the floor, and there before her stood Fenist the Falcon himself, as handsome a youth as ever was born. They spoke lovingly to one another, and the two elder sisters heard them and called out: "Whom are you talking to, sister?" "To myself." "Well, then, open the door!" At this Fenist the Falcon struck the floor and turned into a feather, and the youngest sister picked it up and put it in the box. She opened the door, and the elder sisters came in. They looked here and they looked there but found no one, and as soon as they had left, the youngest daughter opened the window and said: "Fly, my feather, to the open field and bide there for a time!" And the feather turned into a falcon and away it flew.

On the following night Fenist the Falcon came flying back to see his beloved again and they began talking happily to one another, and the two elder sisters heard them and at once ran to tell their father about it. "Someone comes to our sister's chamber at night, he is there now talking to her!" they said. The father got up from bed and hurried to her chamber, but Fenist the Falcon had turned into a feather and was in the box and out of sight when he came in. The father was very angry with his two elder daughters. "You are wicked maids, both, to be spreading such tales!" said he. "Look to yourselves and leave your sister in peace!"

But this did not stop the two elder sisters who decided to use cunning in order to catch whoever it was kept coming to their younger sister's chamber. They waited till it was dark, and, moving a ladder up to the window of her chamber, stuck a large number of sharp needles into the pane. Night came, and Fenist the Falcon flew up to the window, but though he beat against the pane till his wings were cut and bleeding he could not get into his beloved's chamber. "Farewell, fair

maid!" said he. "If ever you want to see me, seek me beyond the thrice-nine lands in the thrice-ten kingdom. But you shall not find me till you have worn out three pairs of iron shoes, broken three iron staffs and eaten three stone loaves!" But the maid slept, and though she heard these chilling words through her sleep, she could not wake up.

Dawn came, she rose and looked out of the window, and, seeing the needles stuck into the pane and the blood dripping down from them, threw up her hands in dismay. "Heavens! My sisters tried to kill Fenist the Falcon," cried she. And she at once got together a few belongings and left the house. She ran to a smithy, had three pairs of iron shoes and three iron staffs made for himself, and, taking along three stone loaves, set out to seek Fenist the Falcon.

On and on she walked, and she had worn out a pair of iron boots, broken an iron staff and eaten a stone loaf when she saw a little hut standing before her. She knocked at the door and said, "Please, Master, please, Mistress, do let me in for the night!" and an old woman let her in. "You are welcome to spend the night in my house, fair maid!" said she. "Whither are you bound?" "I am seeking Fenist the Falcon, Grandma." "It's a long way that lies ahead of you, my dear!" Morning came, and the old woman said: "Go to see my middle sister, and she will help you. Here is a present for you: a stool of silver and a spindle of gold. You will sit down on the stool and spin some tow, and a gold thread will come running out." Then she brought out a ball of yarn, sent it rolling along the road and told the maid to follow it. The maid thanked her and set off after the ball of yarn.

Whether a short or a long time passed nobody knows, but she had worn out a second pair of boots, broken a second staff and eaten a second stone loaf when the ball of yarn brought her to another little hut. She knocked at the door and said. "Please, Master, please, Mistress, do let me in for the night!" and an old woman let her in. "You are welcome to spend the night in my house, fair maid," said she. "Whither are you bound?" "I am seeking Fenist the Falcon, Grandma." "It's a long way you have before you!"

Morning came, and the old woman gave the maid a platter of silver and an egg of gold for a present and told her that she was to go to see her elder sister. "She will know where Fenist the Falcon is to be found!" said she.

The maid bade the old woman goodbye and off she set on her way. On and on she walked, and she had worn out her third pair of iron boots, broken her third iron staff and eaten her last stone loaf when the ball of yarn rolled up to a little hut. She knocked at the door and said, "Please, Master, please, Mistress, do let me in for the night!" and an old woman let her in. "Come inside, my dear, you are welcome to spend the night in my house," said she. "Whither are you bound?" "I am seeking Fenist the Falcon, Grandma." "It will not be easy to get to him," said the old woman, and she told the maid that Fenist the Falcon now lived in such-and-such a town and that he was maried to a wafer-maker's daughter. Morning came, and the old woman said: "Here is a present for you, fair maid: a frame of gold and a needle. All you must do is hold the frame, and the needle will do the needlework all by itself. And now go with God and take up service with the wafer-maker."

No sooner said than done. The maid found the house where the wafer-maker lived, and, coming inside, offered to take up service with her. The wafer-maker hired her and was very pleased she had, for the maid was a quick worker who kept the stove hot, brought in water and cooked their meals, and did it all quickly and well. "God be thanked!" said the wafer-maker to her daughter. "We have got ourselves a servant who is hard-working and who does everything without having to be told." Her chores finished, the maid brought out her silver stool and her gold spindle and began to spin. And as she spun the tow, a thread came running out, and not a plain thread, either, but a gold one. Seeing this, the wafer-maker's daughter said: "Please, fair maid, won't you sell me your playthings?" "Well, I might at that!" "And what do you ask for them?" "I ask for no money. Just let me spend the night in your husband's chamber." To this the wafer-maker's daughter agreed. "No harm can come of it," said she to herself. "With the help of the spindle my mother and I will get rich. And as for my husband, I can give him a sleeping potion so that he will not wake till morning."

Now, Fenist the Falcon was away at the time. He roamed the skies all day and only came back home in the evening. They sat down to eat, and though the maid kept looking at him as he served, he did not recognize her. The wafer-maker's daughter put a sleeping powder into his drink and sent him off to bed, and then she said to the maid: "Go to his chamber and keep the flies away from him!" There sat the maid waving the flies away from her beloved's face, and she wept and sobbed as she did so. "Wake up, wake up, Fenist the Falcon, my own dear love!" cried she. "Long did I seek you, and I wore out three pairs of iron shoes, broke three iron staffs and ate three stone loaves before at last I found you!" But Fenist the Falcon slept on and did not wake.

Night passed, and on the following day the maid brought out her silver platter and began rolling the gold egg over it, and more and more gold eggs appeared on it. The wafer-maker's daughter saw this and said: "Do sell me your playthings, fair maid!" "Well, I might at that!" "And what do you ask for them?" "I ask for no money. Just let me spend the night in your husband's chamber." "Very well, if that's what you want!" Now, Fenist the Falcon was away roaming the skies again, and he only came back toward evening. They sat down to eat their supper, but though the maid kept looking at him as she served, he did not recognize her and it was as though he had never known her. The wafer-maker's daughter gave him a sleeping potion again, put him to bed and sent the maid to keep the flies away

111

from him, and this time, too, though the maid wept and sobbed and tried to wake him, he slept on and did not hear her.

The third day came, and the maid sat there holding the gold frame and watched the needle embroider, making as pretty a pattern as is rarely to be seen! The widow's daughter could not take her eyes from it. "Please, fair maid, sell me your playthings!" she said. "Well, I might at that!" "And what do you ask for them?" "I ask for no money. Just let me spend the night in your husband's chamber." "Very well, if that's what you want!" Evening came, and Fenist the Falcon came flying home. His wife gave him a sleeping potion, put him to bed and then sent the maid to keep the flies away from him. The maid sat there waving the flies away and weeping bitterly, and she kept saying over and over again through her tears: "Come, wake up, Fenist the Falcon, my own dear love, for I am here at your side! Long did I seek you, and I wore out three pairs of iron shoes, broke three iron staffs and ate three stone loaves before I found you at last!" But Fenist the Falcon slept on and never heard her.

The maid wept and sobbed and tried to wake him time and again, but it was not till a tear of hers fell on his cheek that he woke at last. "Something burnt my cheek!" he said. "I am here beside you, Fenist the Falcon," said the maid. "And I wore out three pairs of iron shoes, broke three iron staffs and ate three stone loaves before I found you. For three nights did I stand over you calling your name, but you slept on and never woke." Then it was that Fenist the Falcon knew who stood before him and was filled with such joy as cannot be described! They decided to go away together and left there and then, and when morning came and the wafer-maker's daughter rose, she could find neither her husband nor the maid. She rushed to her mother's chamber and told her about it, and the wafer-maker had her horses harnessed and rode after the runaways. She went everywhere and spoke to everyone, even paying the three old women a visit, but Fenist the Falcon had vanished without a trace and she could not find him.

Fenist the Falcon brought his beloved to her parents' house, he struck the ground and turned into a feather, and the maid picked it up, put it in her bosom and went to see her father. "Ah, my child, it is you!" the father cried. "And I thought I would never see you again. Where have you been all this time?" "Far, far away, Father." Now, it was holy week just then, and the father and his two elder daughters were preparing to go to church for the early morning service. "Won't you join us, my dear?" said he to the youngest daughter. "It's such a happy day for us!" "But I have nothing to wear, Father." "You can put on one of our dresses," her sisters offered. "Ah, no, sisters, your dresses are too fine for me, I think I had better stay home."

Off they went to church, and no sooner had they left than the maid took out her feather and let it drop to the floor, and it turned into Fenist the Falcon, the most handsome youth that ever was born! He leaned out of the window and whistled, and lo!—there before them lay the finest of clothes and of jewels and a coach of gold stood at the door. They put on the clothes and the jewels, and, getting into the coach, drove to the church. They came inside and placed themselves where all could see them, and the townsfolk, who took them to be a prince and a princess, marvelled at the sight of them and asked themselves where it was they could have come from. They left the church before anyone else did, when the service was drawing to a close, and drove home. And no sooner were they there than the coach vanished and so did all the fine clothes and jewels, and Fenist the Falcon turned into a feather. By and by the father came home with his two daughters, and the daughters said: "Ah, sister, a pity you did not come with us! A most handsome prince and a most beautiful of princesses were in church today!"

The next day the same thing happened, but on the third day the father, who came out of the church just as Fenist the Falcon and his bride were getting into the coach, saw it drive up to his house and vanish. He was no sooner home than he asked his youngest daughter if she had seen it. "There's nothing for it but to tell you all!" said she.

She brought out the feather and let it drop to the floor, and it turned into Fenist the Falcon.

Fenist the Falcon and the maid were married, and theirs was the richest wedding that ever was!

I was there and drank ale and wine, but all of it ran down this beard of mine. At the feast till morn I meant to stay, for my spirits were high and my heart was gay, but a cap and a basket were put on my head, and I found myself in the street instead!

Translated by Irina Zheleznova

Elena the Wise

In a certain kingdom, in a certain realm there was once a soldier who happened to be standing guard by a stone tower one night. The door to it was locked and sealed, but just as midnight struck, the soldier seemed to hear someone calling to him from inside the tower. "Who is that calling me?" the soldier asked. "It is I, an evil spirit!" came the reply. "For thirty years have I been kept in the tower, and I haven't had anything to eat or drink in all that time." "What do you want of me?" "Set me free, and I will come to your help if ever you have need of me. All you have to do is think of me, and I will be there beside you the same moment." The soldier at once broke both the seal and the lock and opened the door, and the evil spirit flew out of the tower and up to the sky and vanished as fast as a flash of lightning. "What have I done!" thought the soldier. "All my years of service have gone for nothing. I will be arrested, court-martialled and may even be made to run the gauntlet. I had better go while the going is good." And he threw down his gun and knapsack and went off he knew not where.

He walked for a day, and another, and a third and was very, very hungry, but as there was nothing to eat or drink, he sat down by the wayside and burst into tears. "Fool that I am!" said he to himself. "I served the king for ten years and was given three pounds of bread to eat every day, and look what I've done—run away only to starve to death. It was that evil spirit, he's to blame for it!" And no sooner had he thought of him than there was the evil spirit before him. "Cood

114

day to you, soldier!" said he. "Why so sad?" "How can I help it when I haven't had anything to eat for three days!" "Oh, is that all!" said the evil spirit, and he rushed away only to come back again at once, bringing all sorts of foods and drinks with him. The soldier ate and drank, and when he had had his fill, the evil spirit begged him to come and live in his house. "You will have an easy time of it there," said he. "You will feast and make merry whenever you have a mind to and your only duty will be to keep an eye on my daughters and see that they don't get into mischief." To this the soldier agreed, and the evil spirit lifted him up from the ground and to the sky and carried him off beyond the thrice-nine lads to the thrice-ten realm. It was there, in a house of white stone, that the evil spirit's three daughters lived, and they were fair maids all three.

The evil spirit bade his daughters feed the soldier well and do as he told them to and himself flew away to do evil. And what else could be expected of him! Don't we all know that evil spirits never stay in one place but roam the earth sowing confusion in people's hearts and putting them up to sinful deeds. The soldier stayed with the three maids, and a better life no man could wish for! Only one thing grieved him, and that was that the three maids would leave the house every night without telling him where they went. He tried asking them about it, but they would tell him nothing. "Never mind!" said the soldier to himself. "I will stay awake all night if I have to but I'll find out where it is they go."

Evening arrived and the soldier went to bed and pretended to be asleep. Then, at an hour when the three maids usually left the house, he rose, crept up to their sleeping chamber and looked through the keyhole. What was his surprise when he saw them spread a carpet on the floor, strike it, turn into pigeons and fly out through the window. "Never have I seen the like!" thought the soldier. "But that must be a magic carpet and perhaps I can change myself into a bird too!" He ran into the chamber, struck the carpet, and, turning into a robin, flew out of the window after the pigeons. By and by, when he saw them alight in a green meadow, he did the same, and, hiding himself behind a currant bush, peeked out from under it to see what there was to see. Very soon many pigeons came flying up, so many that they covered the meadow from one end to another. After them, setting the sky and the earth aglow, a chariot of gold drawn by six fiery dragons came sweeping through the air, and seated in it was Elena the Wise, a maid fair beyond compare! She stepped out of the chariot, placed herself on a gold throne that stood in the middle of the meadow and began calling the pigeons to her side one after another and showing them how to do all sorts of magic tricks. This done, she sprang into the chariot and was off in a trice!

All of the pigeons now rose into the air and flew back to wherever it was they had come from, and the robin followed the three sisters and soon found himself back in their chamber again. The pigeons struck the carpet and got back their

116

proper shape, and the robin did the same and got back his. "Where have you been?" the three maids asked him. "In the same place as you. I flew after you to the green meadow, I saw the lovely princess on her throne of gold and I watched her show you how to do all kinds of magic tricks." "Well, it's your good luck that you're still alive! For the princess was none other than Elena the Wise, our ruler and queen. Had she had her book of magic with her she would have known it was you in a robin's shape and would have put you to death. Beware, soldier! Do not fly to the green meadow again or try to see Elena the Wise if you want to stay alive." But the soldier would not listen to them. As soon as night came he struck the carpet, turned into a robin, flew to the green meadow and hid under a currant bush. Elena the Wise came there in her chariot and he watched her and marvelled at her beauty. "If only I could marry her, there would be nothing left for me to wish for!" thought he. "I think I'll fly after her and find out where she lives."

And as soon Elena the Wise got into her chariot and swept to the sky in it, the robin flapped his wings and flew after her. Elena the Wise arrived at the door of her palace, which was very beautiful, and her women and maids hurried out to meet her and led her inside. And the robin flew into the garden, and, lighting on the branch of a tree that grew under the window of Elena the Wise's sleeping chamber, began to sing. It was a sad song and he sang so piteously that Elena the Wise never closed an eye and listened to him the whole night through. Dawn arrived, the sun rose in the sky, and she called out in a loud voice: "Come, my women and maids, hurry and go to the garden and catch the robin for me!" The women and maids rushed out into the garden, but they were old and slow, and the robin flitted from bush to bush, and though he did not fly far, would not let himself be caught.

Filled with impatience, Elena the Wise ran out into the garden to try and catch the robin herself. She came up to the bush on which he had perched, and, much to her surprise, the robin did not try to fly away but sat there with folded wings as if waiting for her to seize him. Elena the Wise was overjoyed. She lifted the bird gently off the branch, carried him into the palace and put him in a gold cage which she hung in her chamber. The day passed, the sun sank in the sky, and Elena the Wise flew to the green meadow. But she was soon back, and, taking off her robe, lay down on her bed. And so lovely was she that the robin trembled at the sight of her, and as soon as she was asleep, took the shape of a fly, flew out of the cage, struck the floor and turned back into a soldier again. He came up to the bed in which Elena the Wise lay sleeping and stood there gazing at her, but then, unable to stop himself, bent and planted a kiss on her honey-sweet lips. Elena the Wise stirred, and, seeing that she was about to wake, he turned into a fly, flew back into the cage and took the robin's shape.

Elena the Wise opened her eyes and looked about her, but, seeing no one, told herself that she had dreamt it all, turned over and fell asleep again. The soldier could not contain himself and kissed her a second and then a third time, and Elena the Wise, who was a light sleeper, woke after every kiss. After the third kiss she got out of bed and said: "This can't be just a dream, I think I had better look in my book of magic." And no sooner had she looked in the book than she knew that sitting in the cage was not a bird but a young man in a bird's shape. "You boor!" cried she. "Come out of the cage at once! You will pay with you life for trying to trick me."

It could not be helped, and the robin flew out of the cage, struck the floor and became a soldier again. He fell on his knees before Elena the Wise and begged her to forgive him. "A villain like you deserves no mercy!" said Elena the Wise, and she summoned a headsman and ordered him to chop off the soldier's head. A scaffold at once appeared before her, and the headsman, a great giant of a fellow, seized the soldier, threw him to the ground, and, pressing down his head with one hand, raised high his axe with the other. Elena the Wise had only to wave her kerchief, and the soldier's head would roll off his shoulders. "O fairest of princesses, allow me to sing a song before I die!" the soldier begged with tears in his eyes. "Oh, very well! Sing your song and get it over with!" said Elena the Wise. The soldier began to sing, and so sad was his song that Elena the Wise felt sorry for him and could hardly stop herself from bursting into tears. "I give you ten hours," said she. "If during that time you will find yourself a hiding place that I will be unable to discover, I shall marry you: if not, you shall die."

The soldier left the palace and wandered off into a thick forest. He sat down under a bush there and gave himself up to sorrowful thoughts. "It's all because of you, evil spirit, that I am in such straits!" said he with a sigh. And no sooner were the words out of his mouth than the evil spirit appeared before him. "What can I do for you, soldier?" he asked. "Nothing, for my end has come!" the soldier said. "Where can I hide Elena the Wise!" At this the evil spirit struck the ground and turned into a grey-winged eagle. "Get on my back, soldier, I will carry you beyond the clouds in the sky!" said he. The soldier got on the eagle's back, and the eagle soared to the sky and hid behind a thundercloud. Five hours went by, and Elena the Wise looked into her book of magic and saw the eagle and the soldier on his back as clearly as if they were there before her. "Come down to the ground, eagle!" she called. "You cannot hide from me."

The eagle came down to the ground, and the soldier felt more sad than ever. "What am I to do now? Where can I hide!" said he. "I will help you, never you fear!" said the evil spirit. He struck the soldier on the cheek, turned him into a pin and himself into a mouse, and, stealing into the palace, found the book of magic and stuck the pin in it.

Another five hours went by, and Elena the Wise opened the book, but though she turned the pages and gazed at each in turn, there was nothing there for her to see. Elena the Wise flew into a temper and flung the book into the stove, but the pin fell out of it, and, no sooner had it touched the floor, than it turned into the soldier again. Seeing him so tall and handsome, for tall and handsome he was, Elena the Wise smiled and took his hand. "I am wise, but you are wiser still!" said she. And they were married then and there and lived happily ever after.

Translated by Irina Zheleznova

The Prophetic Dream

There was once a merchant who had two sons, Dmitri and Ivan. One night, when their father was giving them his blessing, he said: "If you should have a dream tonight, my children, you must tell me it in the morning. He who conceals his dream will be punished." The next morning the elder son came and told his father: "I dreamed that brother Ivan was flying o'er the sky on twelve eagles, Father; and that your favourite sheep was missing." "And you, Ivan, what did you dream?" "I cannot tell!" Ivan replied. No matter how his father urged him, he remained firm, meeting all remonstrances with: "I cannot tell!" The merchant grew angry, summoned his stewards and bade them take the recalcitrant son, strip him naked and tie him to a post on the highroad.

The stewards seized Ivan and bound him naked to a post as they had been bidden. The good youth fared badly: he was scorched by the sun, bitten by mosquitoes and tormented by hunger and thirst. The king's son happened to be driving along the highroad. He saw the merchant's son, took pity on him and bade them untie him. Then he dressed him in his own robes, took him back to the palace and asked of him: "Who tied you to the post?" "My father was angry with me." "What had you done wrong?" "I refused to tell him my dream." "How stupid of your father to punish you so harshly for such a trifle... What was your dream?" "I cannot tell you, my prince!" "You cannot tell me? I saved your life, and you would insult me? Tell me at once, or it will be the worse for you." "I could not tell my father, and I cannot tell you!" The prince ordered him to be cast into a dungeon. Straightway the soldiers came and threw him into a stone cell, the poor soul.

A year passed, and the prince resolved to marry. He set off for a distant land to woo Elena the Fair. Now the prince had a sister, and not long after his departure she happened to be walking near the dungeon. Ivan saw her through the window and shouted in a loud voice: "Take pity, Princess, and let me out. I may be of service! I know the prince has gone to woo Elena the Fair, but without me he will not marry her, only lose his head. You must have heard how cunning Elena the Fair is and how many suitors she has already sent to their doom." "Are you ready to help the prince?" "I would gladly, but my falcon wings are tied." The princess ordered him to be released from the dungeon forthwith. Then Ivan the merchant's son chose him some companions, and there were twelve of them altogether counting Ivan, as alike as blood brothers in height, voice and hair. Then they put on identical cloaks, sewn to the same pattern, mounted their trusty steeds and set off on their way.

They rode for one day, then another and a third. On the fourth day they came to a dense forest and heard some terrible cries. "Stay here, lads!" said Ivan. "Wait while I go to see what the din is about." He leapt off his horse and ran into the forest. There he saw three old men quarreling in a glade. "Good day to you, old men! Why are you quarreling?" "Ah, callow youth! We were left three magic objects by our father, an invisible cap, a flying carpet and a pair of seven-league boots. We have been quarreling for seventy years and still cannot decide how to share them out." "Shall I decide for you?" "Please be so kind!" So Ivan the merchant's son drew his bow, took three arrows and sent them speeding in different directions. He bade one old man run to the right, another to the left and the third straight ahead. "The first to bring back an arrow will get the invisible cap, the second will have the flying carpet, and the third the seven-league boots." The old men ran off after the arrows, and Ivan the merchant's son took the magic objects and returned to his companions. "Let your horses loose, lads," he said, "and mount the flying carpet with me."

So they mounted the flying carpet and sped to the realm of Elena the Fair. Arriving at her capital, they alighted by the city gates and went in search of the prince. They found his chambers. "What can I do for you?" asked the prince. "Take us, trusty youths, into your service. We shall be your servants loyal and true." The prince took them into his service, appointing one to be the cook, another the groom, and so on. That very day the prince donned his best clothes and went to present himself to Elena the Fair. She greeted him warmly, plying him with all manner of fine food and drink, then asked him: "Tell me truly,

Prince, why you have honoured us with this visit." "I have come to woo you, Elena the Fair. Will you be my wife?" "Perhaps I will, indeed. Only first you must perform three tasks. Succeed and I shall be yours, but if you do not your head is for the chopping block." "Tell me the first task." "I shall have something with me tomorrow. What it is I will not say. So use your wits, Prince, and bring your own to form a pair with my unknown."

The prince returned to his chambers downcast and sad of heart. Ivan the merchant's son asked him: "Why so sad, Prince? What has Elena the Fair done to vex you so? Share your grief with me; that will make it lighter." "Elena the Fair has set me a puzzle that the wisest man in the world could not solve." "Oh, that's nothing to worry about! Say your prayers and go to bed; morning is wiser than evening. We'll settle the matter tomorrow." The prince lay down to sleep, but Ivan the merchant's son donned the invisible cap and the seven-league boots and strode quickly to Elena the Fair's palace: he marched straight into her chamber and listened. Elena the Fair was instructing her favourite chamber-maid: "Take this precious material to the shoemaker and bid him make a slipper for my foot as fast as he can."

The chamber-maid set off as she was told, with Ivan following behind her. The shoemaker got down to work forthwith, made the slipper quicky and placed it on the window-sill. Ivan the merchant's son seized it and slipped it quietly into his pocket. The poor shoemaker just couldn't believe his eyes—his work had vanished right under his nose; he turned the place upside down, but all in vain. "Well, I never!" he thought. "Can it be the devil up to his tricks?" There was nothing for it. He picked up his needle, made another slipper and took it to Elena the Fair. "Fancy taking all that time over the slipper! You are a slow coach!" she said. Sitting down at her work-table, she began embroidering the slipper with gold and trimming it with pearls and precious stones. Straightway Ivan appeared, took out his slipper and copied her. Whatever stone she chose, he took one like it, wherever she placed a pearl, he placed one too. When she had finished, Elena the Fair smiled and said: "What will the prince bring with him tomorrow?" "Just you wait," thought Ivan, "we'll see who outwits whom!"

He returned home and went to bed. The next morning he rose with the dawn, dressed and went to rouse the prince. He woke him and gave him the slipper. "Go to Elena the Fair," he said, "and show her this slipper. This is her first task." The prince washed, attired himself and drove to the palace. A great company was assembled there, all the noblemen and counsellors of the realm. When the prince arrived, the music struck up, the guests rose from their seats, and the guards presented arms. Elena the Fair brought out the slipper embroidered with pearls and precious stones, and smiled mockingly at the prince. Then the

prince said to her: "A fine slipper indeed, but no good at all without a mate! I see I shall have to give you one to match!" So saying, he took the second slipper from his pocket and placed it on the table. The guests clapped loudly and cried: "Well done, Prince! He is worthy to marry our sovereign lady, Elena the Fair." "We shall see!" replied Elena the Fair. "Let him perform the second task."

Late that evening the prince returned home even gloomier than before. "Do not grieve, Prince," said Ivan the merchant's son. "Say your prayers and go to bed; morning is wiser than evening." He put him to bed, then donned the seven-league boots and the invisible cap and hurried to the palace of Elena the Fair. At that very moment she was instructing her favourite chamber-maid: "Go quickly to the poultry yard and bring me a duck." The chamber-maid hurried off to the poultry yard with Ivan following her. She caught a duck, Ivan caught a drake, and they returned by the same path. Elena the Fair sat down at her work-table, took the dusk and bedecked its wings with ribbons and its neck with diamonds. Ivan the merchant's son watched her and did the same with the drake. The next day there were guests and music at the palace as before. Elena the Fair brought out her duck and asked the prince: "Have you guessed my task?" "I have, Elena the Fair! Here is a mate for your duck!" And he brought out the drake. Whereupon the noblemen cried: "Well done, young prince!" He is worthy to take Elena the Fair to be his bride. "Wait, let him perform the third task."

That evening the prince came home so gloomy he could hardly speak. "Do not worry, Prince. Just go to ged; morning is wiser than evening," said Ivan the merchant's son. He quickly donned the invisible cap and the seven-league boots and hurried to Elena the Fair. She got into her carriage and drove like the wind down to the deep blue sea, with Ivan the merchant's son following close behind. Elena the Fair came to the sea and called to her grandfather. The waves surged up and out of the watery depths appeared an old man with a golden beard and silver hair. He came onto the shore: "Hello, granddaughter! It's an age since I last saw you; see if there's anything in my hair, will you?" He put his head on her lap and dozed off happily. Elena the Fair looked carefully at his hair, with Ivan the merchant's soon standing close behind her.

Seeing that the old man had fallen asleep, she pulled three silver hairs from his head; but Ivan the merchant's son pulled out a whole handful. Her grandfather woke up and cried: "Have you taken leave of your senses? That hurts!" "Forgive me, Grandfather dear! It's an age since I combed your hair and it's got all tangled." Her grandfather calmed down and soon began to snore again. This time Elena the Fair pulled three golden hairs from his beard; but Ivan the merchant's son grabbed his beard and nearly pulled it off. The old man gave a terrible howl, leapt up and dived into the sea. "Now the prince is doomed for sure," thought Elena the Fair. "He'll never be able to get the same hairs." The next day the guests assembled once more at the palace. The prince came too. Elena the Fair showed him the three silver and three golden hairs and asked: "Have you ever seen the like before?" "That's nothing. I can give you a whole ball of that, if you like." So saying he handed her a tuft of golden and a tuft of silver hair.

Elena the Fair flounced off to her bed-chamber in a rage and consulted her magic book to find out if the prince had guessed the tasks himself or someone had helped him. The book told her that it was his servant. Ivan the merchant's son, who was so cunning, not he. Returning to the guests, she begged the prince: "Send me your favourite servant." "I have twelve of them." "Send the one called Ivan." "They are all called Ivan." "Then let them all come," said Elena the Fair. "I'll find the guilty one without you," she thought to herself. The prince gave the order, and straightway his servants loyal and true, the twelve trusty young men, appeared in the palace; all alike in appearance, height, voice and hair. "Which of you is in charge?" asked Elena the Fair. "Me!" "Me!" they all shouted. "This will be no easy matter," she thought and bade them serve eleven ordinary goblets and the gold one from which she always drank. Then she filled the goblets with good wine and bade the young men partake of it. Not one of them picked up an ordinary goblet. They all reached for the gold one and began to snatch it from one another, making a great din and spilling the wine.

Seeing that her ruse had failed, Elena the Fair ordered the young men to be given food and drink and put to bed in the palace. That night, when they were fast asleep, she went to them with her magic book, consulted it and straightway found out which one was Ivan. Then she took a pair of scissors and cut off his forelock. "I shall recognise him by this tomorrow and have him executed." Next morning Ivan the merchant's son awoke, put his hand to his head and found that his forelock had been cut off. He jumped out of bed and woke his companions. "Up you get, lads, there's trouble brewing! Take some scissors and cut off your forelocks." An hour later Elena the Fair summoned them and began to look for Ivan the merchant's son. But wonder of wonders! The whole bunch of them had their forelocks cut off! She was so angry that she took her magic book and threw it in the stove. After that she could prevaricate no longer and had to marry the prince. The wedding was a gay affair; for three whole days the people revelled, for three whole days the inns and taverns held open house—and all who liked could eat and drink there at the state's expense.

When the feasting was over, the prince set off home with his young bride, sending the twelve young men on ahead. Outside the city gates they unrolled the magic carpet, mounted it and flew up high above the clouds. On and on they sped until they reached the dense forest where they had left their trusty steeds. No sooner had they alighted from the magic carpet, than the first old man came running up with an arrow. Ivan the merchant's son gave him the invisible cap. Hot on his heels came the second old man and received the magic carpet, then the third, who got the seven-league boots. Then said Ivan to his companions: "Saddle your horses, lads, it is time we were on our way." They found their horses, saddled them and rode off to their native land. Straightway they went to the princess. She was overjoyed to see them and asked them about her brother, the wedding and if he was coming home soon. "How can I reward you for such a service?" she asked. "Put me back in the dungeon where I was," replied Ivan the merchant's son. All the princess's efforts to dissuade him were in vain, so the soldiers took him back to the dungeon.

A month later the prince arrived with his young bride. They were given a splendid reception: the music played, the cannons fired, the bells rang and the people thronged the streets. All the noblemen and counsellors came to greet the prince; he looked around him and asked: "Where is Ivan, my faithful servant?" "He is in prison," they said. "In prison? Who dared to put him there?" Then the princess told him: "It was you who got angry with him, brother, and had him locked up. You asked him about a dream, and he refused to tell you, remember?" "Was that Ivan?" "Yes, it was. I let him out for a while to go and serve you." The prince bade them fetch Ivan the merchant's son, embraced him and begged his forgiveness for the wrong that had been done to him. "You know, Prince," said Ivan. "I knew all along what was going to happen to you. I saw it in my dream; that was why I could not tell you about it." The prince made him general, bestowed rich estates upon him and let him live in the palace. Ivan the merchant's son summoned his father and elder brother there, too, and they all lived together happily ever after.

Translated by Kathleen Cook

The Mountain of Gold

A merchant' son went on a spree and ended up without a penny in his pocket. So he took a spade and went to the market place to see if anyone would hire him. Along came a rich merchant in a gilded carriage. At the sight of him all the men looking for work scurried off and hid. Only the youth was left in the square. "Do you want a job, my lad? Come and work for me," said the rich merchant. "Gladly, that is why I have come here." "What shall I pay you?" "A hundred rubles a day will be enough!" "Why so much?" "If it's too much, find someone cheaper. You saw how the man looking for work ran away when you appeared." "Very well, come to the jetty tomorrow." Next morning the youth went to the jetty, where the merchant had been waiting for some time. They got into a boat and sailed out to sea.

On and on they sailed until they saw an island with high mountains and something blazing brightly on the shore. "Is that a fire?" asked the youth. "No, it is my palace of gold." They landed and went ashore. The rich merchant was met by his wife and daughter who was fair as fair, beyond compare. They greeted one another and went to the palace, taking the new workman with them. Then they sat down at table and began to eat, drink and make merry. "Come what may, we'll feast today and get to work tomorrow," said the merchant. Now the youth was a good-looking lad, tall, broad-shouldered and ruddy. He pleased the fair maiden greatly. She slipped away to another chamber, called him to her secretly

and gave him a flint and steel, saying: "Take this to help you when you're in trouble."

The next day the rich merchant went off with his workman to the mountain of gold, up which you could neither climb nor crawl. "Let's drink first," he said, giving the youth a sleeping draught. The youth drank it and fell fast asleep. Then the merchant drew out a knife, killed and gutted an old nag, sewed up the sleeping lad and his spade in the horse's belly and went to hide in the bushes. All of a sudden the jet-black ravens with beaks of steel swooped down, seized the carcass, flew up the mountain with it and bagan to feast. They polished off the horse and were about to start on the youth, when he woke up, shooed the jet-black ravens away, looked about him and asked: "Where am I?" "On the mountain of gold," replied his master. "Pick up your spade and start digging."

So he dug and dug, tossing down the gold, while the merchant loaded it onto carts. By evening there were nine cartloads ready. "That's enough!" shouted his master. "Thank you for your labours and farewell!" "But what about me?" "That's your look-out! Ninety-nine of you have perished up there on the mountain; you will make the hundredth!" said the merchant and off he rode. "What am I to do?" thought the youth. "There is no way of getting down. I shall die of hunger." He stood on the mountain, the jet-black ravens with beaks of steel hovering over him, waiting for their prey. Thinking back about how it had come to pass, he suddenly remembered that the fair maiden had given him the flint and steel, saying "Take this to help you when you're in trouble."

"Those words were not in vain! Let's have a try." The youth took out the flint and steel, struck it and out jumped two strapping young men: "What is your wish, master?" "Take me down the mountain to the seashore." No sooner had he uttered this, than they picked him up and bore him safely down the mountain.

The youth was walking along the seashore, when he saw a boat sailing past the island. "Ahoy, there, good mariners. Take me on board with you." "No, lad! We have no time to stop. It would cost us a hundred leagues." All of a sudden, as the boat sailed on past the island, it was buffeted by strong winds and a terrible storm arose. "That was no ordinary man," cried the mariners. "We'd best return and take him on board." So they turned back to the island, stopped by the shore, took the youth on board and carried him to his native town.

By and by the youth took a spade, went to the market place and waited to be hired. Along came the rich merchant in the golden carriage again. At the sight of him all the others scurried away and hid. Only the youth was left. "Come and work for me," the rich merchant said to him. "Gladly, sir, but it will cost you two hundred rubles a day." "Why so much?" "If it's too much, go and get someone cheaper. You saw how all the men waiting for work ran away when you appeared." "Oh, very well. Come to the jetty tomorrow."

Next morning they met at the jetty, got into a boat and sailed to the island. There they made merry one day, and went to the mountian of gold the next. When they arrived, the rich merchant handed his workman a goblet, saying: "First have a drink!" "Wait, sir! You are the master, you should drink first. Let me pour you some of my own." The youth had brought a sleeping draught; he poured a full glass and handed it to the rich merchant, who drank it and fell into a deep slumber. Then the youth cut open and gutted the oldest nag, sewed up his master and the spade in the horse's belly and hid in the bushes.

All of a sudden the jet-black ravens with beaks of steel swooped down, seized the carcass, flew up the mountain with it and began to feast. The rich merchant woke up and looked about him. "Where am I?" he asked. "On the mountain. Take the spade and start digging. If you dig a lot I'll teach you how to get down." The rich merchant picked up the spade and dug and dug until there were twelve cartloads of gold. "That's enough," said the youth. "Thank you for your labours and farewell!" "But what about me?" "That's your look-out. Ninety-nine of you have perished up there on the mountain; you will make the hundredth!" Taking the twelve cartloads, the youth went to the palace of gold, married the rich merchant's fair daughter, took possession of all his wealth and went with the whole family to live in the capital. And the rich merchant was left on the mountain, where the jet-black ravens with beaks of steel pecked him to death.

Translated by Kathleen Cook

A Cunning Trade

There was once a man and his wife, and they had a son. The father was very poor. He wanted to apprentice his son to a trade so that the boy would be a comfort to his parents, a support to them in old age, and pray for them when they were dead and gone. But what can you do without cash! He trudged round town after town with him. Surely someone would take the lad on; but no, no one would teach him a trade without payment. The father went home, moaned and groaned with his wife, bewailing his poverty, and again took his son to town. No sooner had they arrived, than they met a man who asked the father: "Why so downcast, my man?" "How can I help it," replied the father. "I've been trudging around with my son, but no one will teach him a trade without payment, and I have no money." "Give him to me," said the man. "In three years I will teach him all my skills. And in three years' time, on this very day and at this very hour, you must come and collect him. But mind you are not late. If you arrive on time and rcognise your son, you may take him back. But if not, he will stay with me." The father was so overjoyed that he did not ask who the man was, where he lived and what he was proposing to teach his son. He gave him the lad and went away. He returned home happily and told his wife the glad news. But the man he had met was a sorcerer.

Three years passed. The father had forgotten exactly when he had handed over his son, and did not know what to do. The day before the three years were up, his son flew to him in the form of a bird, struck the mound of earth outside

131

and came into the house as a strapping young man. He greeted his father and said that the three years were up tomorrow and he must come and fetch him. Then he told him where to go and how to recognise him. "I am not my master's only apprentice," he said. "There are eleven more youths who must stay with him forever, because their parents did not recognise them. If you do not recognise me, I shall be the twelfth. When you come for me tomorrow, our master will let the twelve of us loose as white doves, alike as peas in a pod, with the same feathers, tail and head. But take heed. We will all fly high up, but I will fly higher than the rest. My master will ask you if you recognise your son. And you must point to the dove that is higher than the rest. After that he will drive out twelve stallions, alike as peas in a pod with their manes all combed on the same side. Take heed as you walk past the stallions, for I shall paw slightly with my right hoof. My master will ask you again if you recognise your son. And you must point to me. After that he will bring out twelve strapping youths, alike as peas in a pod, with the same height, hair and voices, the same faces and the same dress. As you walk past the youths, take heed, for a little fly will settle on my right cheek. The master will ask you again if you recognise your son. And you must point to me."

So saying he bade farewell to his father and walked out of the house, then struck the mound of earth, turned back into a bird and flew off to his master. In the morning the father got up, made himself ready and went off to fetch his son. He came to the sorcerer. "Well, my friend," said the sorcerer. "I have taught your son all my skills. But if you do not recognise him, he must stay with me forever." Whereupon he let loose twelve white doves, alike as peas in a pod with the same feathers, tail and head, and asked: "Do you recognise your son?" How could he recognise his son, when they were all alike! He looked hard, and when one dove flew higher than the rest he pointed at it. "I do believe that's him!" "You are right!" said the sorcerer.

Then he let loose twelve stallions, alike as peas in a pod, with their manes all combed on the same side. The father walked round the stallions and took a good look at them, and the sorcerer asked: "Now then, my friend! Do you recognise your son?" "Not yet. Wait a little." When he saw one stallion paw the ground with his right hoof, he pointed at it: "I do believe that's him." "You are right!" The third time out came twelve strapping youths, alike as peas in a pod with the same height, hair and voices, and the same faces as if born of one mother. The father walked past them and noticed nothing, then again and still he noticed nothing, but as he walked past a third time he saw a small fly on the right cheek of one youth and said: "I do believe that's him." "You are right!" So there was nothing for it. The sorcerer gave the old man his son, and the two of them set off home.

As they walked along they saw a fine gentleman riding in a carriage. "I shall turn myself into a dog, father," said the son. "The gentleman will want to buy me. Sell me to him, but keep my collar, or I shall never come back again." So saying he struck the ground and turned into a dog. The fine gentleman saw the father leading a dog and began to bargain for it. It was not so much the dog he wanted, as the smart collar. The gentleman offered a hundred rubles for the dog, but the father wanted three hundred. After a lot of haggling the gentleman bought the dog for two hundred. When the father began to take off the collar, the fine gentleman protested for all he was worth. "I didn't sell the collar," said the father, "I only sold the dog." "Fiddlesticks!" cried the gentleman. "Whoever buys the dog, gets the collar as well." The father thought hard (it was true that you didn't buy a dog without a collar) and let him have it collar and all. The gentleman sat the dog beside him, and the old man took the money and set off home.

All of a sudden as the gentleman was riding along, a hare suddenly popped out and raced past. "Shall I send the dog after the hare and watch it run like billy-ho?" thought the fine gentleman. No sooner did he let it go, than the dog raced off in the opposite direction straight into the forest. The gentleman waited a long time for it, then went on his way empty-handed. And the dog turned back into the strapping youth. The father trudged home, wondering how he dared show his face there and how to tell the old woman what had happened to their son. Then the son caught him up. "Oh, father," he said. "Why did you sell me with the collar? If we hand't met a hare, I would never have come back, and that would have been the last you saw of me!"

They reached home and settled down there happily. Time passed, how much I cannot say, and one Sunday the son said to his father: "I shall turn into a bird, father, and you take me to market and sell me. Only don't sell the cage, or I shall never come back again." He struck the ground and turned into a bird. The old man put it in a cage and took it off to sell. Folk gathered round the man quickly and began making offers for the bird: it was such a nice one.

The sorcerer was there too. He recognised the man straightaway and guessed what kind of bird he had in his cage. The bids were high, but he outbid the lot of them. The man sold him the bird, but would not give him the cage. The sorcerer cajoled and threatened, but the man remained adamant. So he took the bird, wrapped it in a kerchief and went home. "Hey, daughter," he said at home, "I've bought that rascal of ours!" "Where is he then?" The sorcerer unfolded the kerchief with a flourish, but there was no bird. It had flown home ages ago, bless its heart.

Sunday came round again, and the son said to his father: "Today I shall turn into a horse, father. Make sure to sell the horse, but not the bridle, or I shall never come back again." He struck the ground and turned into a horse. His father took it to market to sell. The traders gathered round them. The bids were high, but the sorcerer outbid the lot of them. The man sold him the horse, but would not hand over the bridle. "How can I lead the horse without it?" asked the sorcerer. "Just let me lead it home, then take the bridle if you wish. I have no need of it." Whereupon the traders turned on the man. That wasn't right. If you sold a horse, you sold the bridle with it. There was nothing for it, so the man handed over the bridle.

The sorcerer led the horse home, put it in the stable and tied it tightly to a ring, pulling its head high. The horse had to stand on its hind legs, for its front legs could not reach the ground. "Hey, daughter," the sorcerer cried again. "I've bought that rascal of ours like I did before." "Where is he then?" "Standing in the stable." His daughter ran to see. She felt sorry for the young man and decided to loosen the rein. No sooner had she untied it, than the horse leapt out and raced off like the wind. The daughter ran to her father. "Oh, father, forgive me!" she cried. "I loosened the rein, and the horse has run away!"

The sorcerer struck the ground, turned into a wolf and sped off in pursuit. He drew closer and closer. The horse raced down to the river, struck the ground, turned into a little fish and dived into the water. The wolf pursued it in the form of a pike. The little fish swam on through the water until it reached a jetty where some fair maidens were doing their washing. It turned into a gold ring and rolled under the feet of a merchant's daughter. The merchant's daughter picked up the ring and hid it. Then the sorcerer took on human form again. "Give me back my gold ring," he ordered her.

"Take it," said the girl and threw the ring on the ground.

As it struck the ground, there was a shower of grain. The sorcerer turned into a cockerel and began to peck it up. While he was pecking, one grain turned into a hawk, and the cockerel was in trouble. The hawk finished it off in no time. And, prithee, now my tale is told, a mug of ale, if I might make so bold.

Translated by Kathleen Cook

The White Duck

There was once a prince who married a most beautiful princess, but he had not yet had time to feast his eyes on her to his heart's content or to have enough of talking to and listening to her when the time came for them to part, for he had to go on a far journey. What was to be done! The princess wept and the prince, who kept begging her not to, bade her, since he was leaving her with strangers, never to leave her chambers, to avoid the company of wicked people and to close her ears to wicked talk. This the princess promised to do, and as soon as the prince had gone, she locked herself in her chamber. One day a woman, who seemed a simple and kindly soul enough, came to see the princess. "Why should you eat your heart out!" said she. "Why don't you at least go out for a walk in the garden and have a breath of fresh air?" At first the princess would not hear of it, but then, telling herself that a walk in the garden could do her no harm, she went outside. Now, in the garden was a stream with the freshest, clearest spring water ever seen. "It's very hot today," the woman said, "and the water is nice and cool. So why don't you take a dip?" "No, no, I can't do that!" the princess said, but then she took off her gown and stepped into the water. And the woman at once struck her on the back, and saying "Be a white duck and swim in the water!", turned her into a white duck. After that the witch, for that was what the woman was, took the princess's shape, put on the princess's gown, combed her hair, painted her cheeks and brows and sat down to wait for the prince. By and by a pup yelped, a bell tinkled, and there was the prince at the gate! The witch

136

rushed out to meet him, she embraced and kissed him, and the prince, who was overcome with joy, pressed her to his heart.

And as for the white duck, she laid three eggs, and out of them three babies were hatched, three boys, two of them fine, sturdy little lads, and the third, a tiny little thing. Their mother took good care of them and they grew quickly and were soon splashing about and catching fish, which now became their favourite dish, jumping out on the bank for a look at the lea, a place which they found very pleasant to see, and were nothing loath to make shirts of cloth. "Don't go far, children!" the mother said. But the three boys would not listen to her and with each passing day went farther away. One day they wandered even farther away than usual and found themselves in the prince's courtyard. The witch knew at once who they were and gnashed her teeth in anger. She got them to come inside, gave them food and drink and put them to bed, and then ordered fires to be kindled, kettles to be hung and knives sharpened. The two bigger lads lay down and fell fast asleep, but the third, the tiny one, whom one or the other of them kept always in his bosom lest he catch cold, did not sleep and saw and heard everything. In the middle of the night the witch came to the door of their chamber and called: "Are you asleep, my little ones?" And Tiny called back:

> "We cannot sleep for the thoughts that chill us;
> We dare not sleep, for they mean to kill us—
> Fires are being kindled,
> Kettles are being hung,
> Knives are being sharpened!"

"They're not asleep!" the witch told herself. She went away, took a walk and then came back to the door of their chamber again. "Are you asleep, my little ones?" she called. But Tiny called back again:

> "We cannot sleep for the thoughts that chill us;
> We dare not sleep, for they mean to kill us—
> Fires are being kindled,
> Kettles are being hung,
> Knives are being sharpened!"

"Why is it that one and the same voice answers me?" thought the witch. She opened the door quietly, and, seeing that the two brothers were sound asleep, passed a dead man's hand cut off at the wrist over them so that they might never wake.

In the morning the white duck called to her children, but they did not reply, and her heart told her that evil had befallen them. She flew to the prince's court-yard, and there were her sons, their faces white as snow and their bodies cold as ice, lying side by side. She rushed to them, her wings outspread, and called out in a human voice:

> "Quack-quack, my sons,
> "Quack-quack, my beloved ones,
> In want I reared you,
> With tears I suckled you,

You slept—I lay sleepless,
You ate—I went hungry."

"Did you ever hear the like, Wife?" the prince asked. "The duck is speaking in a human voice." "It only seems so to you," the witch told him. "Ho there, all! Drive the duck out of the yard!" The servants chased the duck away, but it flew round and round and dropped down beside her children again.

"Quack-quack, my sons,
Quack-quack, my beloved ones!"

she called again.

"The witch it was that put you to sleep,
The witch it was with her wicked ways,
For a snake is she and a deadly one...
From you she took your father own,
Your father own and my own dear spouse;
She drowned us all in the river swift,
She turned us all into white-winged ducks,
And herself she lives like a princess true!"

"Ah, so that is the truth of it!" said the prince, and he called to his servants telling them to catch the duck. They rushed to do his bidding, but the duck flew round and round and would not be caught. But when the prince went after her himself she came down of her own free will and dropped into his hands. He took her by the wing and said: "Rise behind me, a white birch! Stand before me, a fair maid!"

And lo!—a white birch rose behind him and a fair maid stood in front of him, and she was none other but his own dear wife.

They then caught a magpie, and, tying two phials to its wings, bade it fill one with living water and the other with talking water. Away flew the magpie and was soon back with the living and the talking water. They sprinkled their sons with the living water, and the lads started and came back to life; they sprinkled them with the talking water, and they began talking and laughing.

And so now the prince has his whole family with him, and they never had cause to shed a tear and prospered the more from year to year. Never more to return was the evil past, and they could be happy together at last. And as for the witch, she was tied to a horse's tail and the horse sent across a field. Where the witch's leg came off, there a poker appeared; where her arm was severed, there lay a rake; where her head rolled down, there a burdock grew up. The birds came flying up, and they pecked the flesh; the winds swept up, and they bore off the bones. And nothing was left of the wicked witch, neither trace nor word nor memory.

Translated by Irina Zheleznova

The Riddle

A peasant was sowing in a field by the high road. The king came riding along, stopped and said to the peasant: "May the good Lord put power to your elbow, my man!" "Thank you, kind sir!" (He did not know it was the king.) "And do you reap much gain from this field?" enquired the king. "Some eighty rubles if the harvest be good." "And what do you do with the money?" "I give twenty rubles in taxes, twenty to repay a debt, twenty as a loan, and throw twenty out of the window." "Tell me, my man, what debt are you repaying, to whom are you lending money and why do you throw twenty rubles out of the window?" "Supporting my father is repaying a debt, feeding my son is giving a loan, and keeping my daughter is throwing money out of the window." "Well said!" exclaimed the king, giving him a handful of silver. He announced who he was and ordered the peasant not to tell the same to any man without his countenance. "No matter who asks, tell no one!"

The king came to his capital and called together his nobles and generals. "Solve this riddle," he said. "By the roadside I saw a peasant sowing a field. I asked him how much gain it yielded and what he did with the money. The man replied that he got eighty rubles from a good harvest; he gave twenty in taxes, twenty to repay a debt, twenty as a loan and threw twenty out of the window. Whoever solves this riddle will be richly rewarded and highly honoured." The noblemen and generals racked their brains, but could not find the answer. Then a

certain nobleman went to the peasant with whom the king had spoken, offered him a pile of silver rubles and asked him how to solve the king's riddle. The man was greatly tempted by the money, took it and told the nobleman all. The nobleman returned to the king and straigtway gave him the answer to his riddle.

The king saw that the peasant had not kept his word and ordered him to be brought to the palace. The man came before the king and confessed right away that it was he who had told the nobleman the answer. "Well, you have only yourself to blame, my man. For such an offence I shall order you to be executed!" "But Your Majesty! I have committed no offence, for it was not without your countenance that I told the nobleman all." So saying the peasnt took from his pocket a silver ruble with the king's head upon it and showed it to the king. "Well said!" exclaimed the king. "That is indeed my countenance." He rewarded the peasant richly and sent him home.

Translated by Kathleen Cook

The Wise Maid
and the Seven Robbers

There was once a peasant who had two sons: the younger son went out into the world and the elder one stayed at home. On his death-bed the father left all he possessed to the son who had stayed at home, and gave the younger son nothing, thinking that his brother would see to it. But when the father died, the elder son buried him and took everything for himself. The younger son came home and wept bitterly at not finding his father alive. Then the elder son said to him: "Father has left everything to me!" He had no children, but his brother, the younger son, had a son and a foster-daughter. So the elder son inherited everything, grew rich and began to trade in fine wares; but the younger son was poor, chopped wood in the forest and sold it at the market. The neighbours pitied him, got togethter and offered him money so that he could set himself up in trade, albeit in trifles. But the poor son was afraid and said to them: "No, good folk, I will not take your money. If I were to trade at a loss, how would I repay the debt?" Then two neighbours thought of a plan to give him the money. One day when the poor man set off to cut firewood, one of them overtook him on the way and said: "I am going on a long journey, friend. Someone has just repaid me three hundred rubles, and I don't know what to do with it! I don't want to go home; take the money for me and look after it, or better still use it to set yourself up in trade. I won't be back for some time. You can pay the money back little by little later."

The poor man took the money home, afraid that he would lose it or his wife would find it and spend it. He racked his brains and hid it in a pot of ash, then went out. While he was away the men who buy up ashes and exhange them for good came. The woman gave them the pot. When the man came home he saw the pot had gone and asked: "Where are the ashes?" "I sold them to the ash-men." The man began to grieve and worry, but said nothing. Seeing that he was distressed, his wife went to him and said: "What misfortune has befallen you? Why are you so downcast?" Then he told her that someone else's money had been hidden in the ashes. The woman was angry, she stamped her foot, burst into tears and wailed: "Why didn't you trust me? I would have hidden it in a better place."

The man set off again for firewood, to sell it at the market and buy some corn. On they way he met the other neighbour, who told him the same story and gave him five hundred rubles to keep. The poor man did not want to take it and kept refusing, but the other man thrust it into his hand and galloped off. The money was in paper notes. The poor man racked his brains about where to put it. In the end he stuffed it into the lining of his cap. When he reached the forest he hung the cap on a fir-tree and began to chop wood. To his misfortune a jackdaw flew up and carried away the cap with the money. The poor man grieved and worried for a while, then resigned himself to his lot and began to live as before, selling firewood and other trifles and just making ends meet. Seeing that some time had passed and the poor man's trade was not prospering his neigbours asked him: "Why is your trade going so badly, brother? Are you afraid of using our money? If that's the case, you'd better give it back." The poor man burst into tears and told them that he had lost the money. The neighbours did not believe him and went to court to get it back. "How can I pass judgement on this case?" pondered the judge. "The man is a harmless fellow with no money to pay back. If I put him in jail, he'll die of hunger!"

The judge sat deep in thought by the window. At that moment some boys where playing in the street outside. One of them, a chirpy lad, said: "I'll be the bailiff. You bring me your petitions and I'll pass judgement on them." So he sat down on a stone, then another boy came up to him and said: "I lent that man some money and he won't pay it back to me. I have come to ask you to judge the matter." "Did you accept the loan?" the bailiff asked the culprit. "Yes." "Then why don't you repay it?" "I've nothing to repay it with, Your Worship." "Listen, petitioner! This man does not deny that he took money from you, but he is not able to pay it back, so give him five or six years to settle the debt. In that time his fortunes may change and he'll repay it with interest. Do you agree?" The boys both bowed to the bailiff: "Thank you, Your Worship! We agree." The judge heard this and was overjoyed, saying: "That boy has given me the answer. I'll tell my petitioner to defer repayment too." At his bidding the rich neighbours agreed to wait for two or three years, by which time the poor man's fortunes might change.

144

So the poor man again went off to the forest for wood. He had only chopped half a cartload when it grew dark. So he decided to spend the night in the forest. "Tomorrow morning I'll go home with a full cartload." Then he looked about for somewhere to sleep. It was a deserted spot with many wild animals. If he lay down beside the horse, the beasts might eat them. So he went into a thicket and climbed a big fir tree. That night seven robbers came to that very spot and said: "Open, doors, open!" Straightway some doors opened up into an underground cave. The robbers stowed away their booty and said: "Close, doors, close!" The doors closed, and the robbers went off for more booty. The poor man saw all this and when it was quiet again all around he climbed down from the tree. "Let's see if the doors will open for me," he thought. No sooner had he said "Open, doors, open!" than they opened wide before him. He went into the cave and saw piles of gold, silver and all manner of precious things lying there. The poor man was overjoyed and set about moving the sacks of money at sunrise. He took the firewood off his cart, loaded it with gold and silver and hurried home.

"There you are, dear husband!" cried his wife. "I was worried to death, wondering what had happened to you. I thought you had been crushed by a tree or eaten by a wild beast." "Don't worry, wife!" said the man happily. "The Lord has been kind to us. I have found some treasure. Help me carry in the sacks." When they had finished, he went to his rich brother, told him what had happened and invited him to come and share the treasure. His brother agreed. Off they went together, found the fir tree and shouted: "Open, doors, open!" The doors opened and they began to drag out the sacks of money. The poor brother filled up his cart and was satisfied, but the rich one wanted more. "You go on ahead, brother," said the rich one. "I'll catch you up rightaway." "Very well! But don't forget to say 'Close, doors, close!'" "I won't forget." The poor brother drove off, but the rich one could not tear himself away. There was too much to take at one go, but he was loath to leave it. He was still there at nightfall. The robbers came, found him in the underground cave and cut off his head; they took the sacks of money off the cart, put the dead brother on it, whipped the horse and let it go. The horse galloped out of the forest and took the dead man home. Then the robber chief cursed the one who had killed the rich brother. "Why did you kill him so soon? We should have found out where he lived first. Lots of our stuff has gone; he must have made several journeys. How can we get it back now?"

"Let the one who killed him find out where he lived," said his second in command.

A little later the robber who had killed him set out to try and find the gold. He marched into the poor brother's shop, bold as brass, bought a few things, saw the shopkeeper was sad, thought for a moment and asked: "Why are you so downcast?" "I had an elder brother, and a terrible thing happened," said the poor brother. "Someone killed him. Two days ago his horse brought him home with his head chopped off, and we buried him today." Seeing that he was on the right track, the robber began asking questions, pretending to be very sorry. He learned that the dead man had left a widow and asked: "Does the poor woman have a roof over her head?" "Yes, a big house!" "Where is it? Show me." The man went and showed the robber his brother's house; the robber took some red paint and painted a sign on the gate. "What's that for?" asked the man. "I'd like to help the poor woman, so I have painted a sign to help me find the house," replied the robber. "Why, friend! My sister-in-law lacks nothing. She lives in plenty, thank the Lord." "And where do you live?" "This is my house." The robber painted the same sign on his gate too. "What's that for?" "I've taken a liking to you," said the robber. "I'll drop in now and then to spend the night. You won't regret it, friend, believe me." The robber returned to the band, and told them what had happened. They agreed to go that night, rob and kill everyone in both houses and get their gold back.

The poor man came home and said: "I've just met a young fellow who put a sign on my gate and said he would drop in now and then to spend the night here. Such a kind soul! He was so sorry about my brother and wanted to help his widow!" His wife and son just listened to him, but his foster-daughter said: "Perhaps you were wrong, father. Perhaps it won't be alright. What if uncle was killed by the robbers, and now they want to get their booty back and have come looking for us? They might turn up and kill the lot of us for it." The man became alarmed: "I might have guessed. I'd never seen him in my life before. Oh, dear! What shall we do?" "Take some paint, father," said the girl, "and paint the same sign on all the gates in the neighbourhood." The man went out and painted the sign on all the gates in the neighbourhood. The robbers came and could not find what they wanted; they went back and beat the first robber for painting signs everwhere. In the end they decided: "We must be dealing with a cunning devil!" A little later they prepard seven barrels; they hid a robber in six of them and filled the seventh with oil.

The first robber set off with the barrels to the poor brother's house. He arrived towards evening and asked it he might stay the night. The brother received him like an old friend. The foster-daughter went into the yard and began to examine the barrels. She opened one and found oil, then tried to open another—but no, she could not. She bent down and put her ear to it. Something was moving and breathing inside it. "Ha, ha," she thought. "Someone's up to nasty tricks!" She came into the house and said: "How shall we entertain our guest, father? Let me stoke up the stove at the back and cook something nice for supper." "Very well." The foster-daughter went and stoked the stove. While she was cooking, she boiled some water and poured it into the barrels, scalding the robbers to death. While her father and the guest had supper, the girl sat at the back waiting to see what would happen. When the master and mistress had gone to sleep, the guest went into the yard and whistled. Nothing stirred. He went up to the barrels and called to his mates. There was no reply. Then he opened the barrels and the steam poured out. Realising what had happened, the robber harnessed the horses and drove off with the barrels.

The foster-daughter locked the gates, woke up the household and told them what had happened. Her father said: "You've saved our lives, my lass. You shall be my son's lawful wife." There was a wedding and a merry feast. The young woman kept urging her father-in-law to sell his old house and buy another. She feared the robbers greatly! Who knows, they might turn up again one day! And so they did. A little later the robber who had brought the barrels dressed up as an officer, came to the poor brother's house and asked if he could stay the night. They took him in, suspecting nothing. But the young woman guessed who it was and said: "Father! It is the robber who came before!" "No, it isn't, lass."

She said nothing more, but before lying down, fetched a sharp axe and put it by her bedside. She did not sleep a wink, but lay awake keeping watch. At dead of night the officer got up, took his sabre and made to cut off her husband's head. Quick as a flash she swung her axe and cut off his right arm, then swung it again and chopped off his head. Now the poor brother could see that his daughter-in-law was a wise lass, indeed. So he did as she said, sold the house and bought an inn. He settled down there and began to do a brisk trade and prosper.

One day his old neighbours, the ones who had lent him money and taken him to court, dropped in. "What are you doing here?" they asked. "It's my house, I've just bought it not long ago." "And a fine house it is too. You must be doing well. Why don't you pay back your debt?" The man bowed and said: "Praise the Lord! He has been kind to me. I found some treasure and will gladly pay you back threefold!" "So be it, friend. Let's celebrate the house-warming." "Let us indeed." So they ate, drank and made merry. Now the house had a fine garden. "Can we take a look at the garden," they asked. "With pleasure, dear sirs. I will take you round it myself." So out they went for a walk in the garden and in a far corner found a pot of ashes. The brother took one look at it and exclaimed: "Dear sirs! This is the very pot that my wife sold." "Well, let's see if the money is still in it." They shook the pot and out fell the money. So the neighbours could see that the man had been telling the truth. "Let's take a look at that tree," they said. "The jackdaw that stole the cap may have built a nest in it." They searched around, saw a nest, got it down with a boathook, and there it was—the very same cap! They pulled out the twigs and found the money. Then the brother paid them what he owed and settled down happily to live a life of plenty.

Translated by Kathleen Cook

The Fortune-Teller

In a certain village there lived an old woman, and she had a son, neither too big nor too small, but not old enough to work in the fields. Things came to such a pass that they had nothing in the larder. So the old woman put on her thinking cap and racked her brains to find a way to make ends meet and have a loaf of bread to eat. She thought and thought, until she had an idea. So she said to the boy: "Go lead away somebody's horses, tether 'em to that there bush and give 'em some hay, then untether 'em again, lead 'em to that there hollow and leave 'em there." Now her son was a smart lad, and no mistake. No sooner did he hear this, than off he went, led away some horses and did what his mother had told him.

For it was said of her that she knew more than ordinary folk and could read the cards now and then when asked.

When the owners saw their horses had gone, they went in search of them, hunting high and low, poor devils, but there was not a sign of them. "What are we to do?" they cried. "We must get a fortune-teller to find 'em for us, even though it means paying through the nose." Then they remembered the old woman and said: "Let's go to her and ask her to read the cards; like as not she'll tell us summit about 'em." No sooner said than done. They went to the old woman and said; "Granny, dear. We have heard say that you know more than ordinary folk. That you can read the cards and tell all from 'em like an open book. Then read 'em for us, dear mistress, for our horses are gone." Then the old woman said to them: "My strength is failing, dear masters! I am forever a-wheezing and a-gasping, sirs." But they replied: "Do as we ask, dear mistress! It is not for naught. We shall reward you for your pains."

Shuffling and coughing, she laid out the cards, peered hard at them and although they told her nothing—what of it; hunger is no brother, it teaches you a thing or two—said: "Well, I never! Look here, sirs! It seems your horses are in that there place, tethered to a bush." The owners were overjoyed, rewarded the old woman for her pains and went to look for their beasts. They came to the bush, but there was no sign of the horses, though you could see where they had been tethered, 'cause part of a bridle was hanging on the bush and there was lots of hay around. They had been there, but now they were gone. The men were grieved, poor devils, and didn't know what to do. They thought it over and went back to the old woman. If she had found out once, she would tell them again.

So they came to the old woman, who was lying on the stove-bed, a-wheezing and a-gasping like goodness knows what was ailing her. They begged her earnestly to read the cards for them again. She pretended to refuse as before, saying: "My strength is failing. I am plagued by old age!"—so that they would give her a bit more for her pains.

They promised to begrudge her nothing if the horses were found and give her more than before. So the old woman climbed down from the stove-bed, shuffling and coughing, laid out the cards again, peered hard at them and said: "Go look for them in that there hollow. That's where they are for sure!" The owners rewarded her handsomely for her pains and set off again to look. They reached the hollow and found their horses safe and sound: so they took them and led them home.

After that the stories spread far and wide about the old woman with second sight who could read the cards and tell you surely what would come to pass. These rumours reached a certain rich gentleman who had lost a chest full of money.

When he heard about the old fortune-teller, he sent his carriage to bring her to him without delay, no matter how poorly she felt. He also sent his two manservants, Nikolasha and Yemelya (it was they who had pinched their master's money). So they came for the old woman, all but dragged her into the carriage by force and set off home.

On the way the old woman began to moan and groan, sighing and muttering to herself: "Oh, dear. If it weren't for no cash and an empty belly I would never be a fortune-teller, riding in a carriage for a fine gentleman to lock me up where the ravens would not take my bones. Alas, alack! No good will come of this!"

Nikolasha overheard her and said: "Hear that, Yemelya! The old girl's talking about us. Looks as if we're for it!" "Steady now, lad," said Yemelya. "Perhaps you just imagined it." But Nikolasha told him: "Listen for yourself, there she goes again." The old woman was scared out of her wits. She sat quiet for a while, then began moaning again: "Oh, dear! If it weren't for no cash and an empty belly this would never have happened!" The lads strained their ears to catch what she was saying. After a bit she went on again about "no cash and an empty belly", blathering all sorts of nonsense. When the lads heard this, they got a real fright. What were they to do? They agreed to ask the old woman not to give them away to their master, because she kept saying: "If it weren't for Nikolasha and Yemelya, this would never have happened." In their excitement the two rascals thought the old woman was talking about Nikolasha and Yemelya, not no cash and an empty belly!

No sooner said than done. They begged the old woman: "Have pity on us, Granny dear, and we'll say prayers for you forever more. Why ruin us and tell the master all? Just don't mention us, keep quiet about it: we'll make it worth your while." Now the old woman was no fool. She put two and two together, and her fear vanished in a trice. "Where did you hide it, my children?" she asked. "It was the Devil himself tempted us to commit such a sin," they wailed. "But where is it?" repeated the old woman. "Where else could we hide it but under the bridge by the mill until the good weather comes." So they reached an agreement and then arrived at the rich gentleman's house. When he saw they had brought the old woman, their master was beside himself with joy. He led her into the house and plied her with all manner of food and drink, whatever she fancied, and when she had eaten and drunk her fill, he asked her to read the cards and find out where his money was. But the old woman had her wits about her and kept saying that her strength was failing and she could hardly stand. "Come now, Granny," said the gentleman. "Make yourself at home, sit down, if you like, or lie down if you don't feel well enough to sit, only read the cards and find out what I asked. And if you can tell me who took my money and I find it again, I'll not only wine and dine you, but reward you handsomely with anything that you fancy."

And so, a-wheezing and a-gasping as if afflicted by some terrible malady, the old woman took the cards, laid them out and peered hard at them, muttering to herself all the time. "Your lost chest is under the bridge by the mill," she said finally.

No sooner had he heard the old woman's words, than the gentleman sent Nikolasha and Yemelya to find the money and bring it to him. He did not know it was they who had taken it.

So they found it and brought it to their master; and their master was so overjoyed to see his money, that he did not count it, and gave the old woman a hundred rubles straightaway and a nice little present besides, promising not to forget her service to him in the future as well. Then, having entertained her lavishly, he sent her home in his carriage and gave her something for the road as well.

On the way Nikolasha and Yemelya thanked the old woman for not betraying them to their master and gave her some money too.

After that the old woman was more famous than ever and settled down to a life of ease with all the bread she wanted, and other fare in abundance, and plenty of livestock too. And she and her son lived and prospered and drank beer and mead. For I was there and drank mead-wine, it touched my lips, but not my tongue.

Translated by Kathleen Cook

Ivan the Fool

There once lived an old man and an old woman who had three sons, two of them clever young men, but the third, who was named Ivan, a fool. The clever sons grazed sheep, but the fool did nothing save sit on the stove and catch flies. One day the old woman made some rye dumplings and she said to the fool: "Here, take these dumplings to your brothers." She filled a pot full of soup and dumplings and gave it to him, and the fool set out for the field. The day was a sunny one, and as soon as he left the village he saw his shadow on the road beside him. "Who is that man walking at my side and never falling a step behind me?" thought he. "He must want some of my dumplings." And he began throwing the dumplings to the shadow one after another. Soon not one was left, but there was the shadow beside him still. "What a glutton!" said the fool, vexed, and he flung the pot at the shadow. The pot broke, and the crocks flew to all sides.

He came to the field empty-handed, and the brothers asked him what he was there for. "I have brought you your dinner," said he. "Where is it, then? Give it to us and be quick about it!" "Well, you see, brothers, a man, a stranger, tagged after me all the way here and ate up everything!" "What man was that?" "There he is, still standing beside me!" The brothers began scolding and beating the fool, they gave him a sound thrashing, and, leaving him to tend the sheep, went home to have their dinner.

The fool began grazing the sheep, and seeing them straying over the field, ran after them. He caught them, one after another, and put out their eyes, and, when

154

he had blinded them all, gathered them round him and sat there looking as pleased as if he had done something praiseworthy. The brothers had their dinner and came back to the field. "What have you done, you fool!" they cried. "Who has put out the sheep's eyes!" "What do they need eyes for!" the fool said. "As soon as you left they strayed all over the field, so I caught them, put out their eyes, and here they are all in a bunch again. And I'm that tired I can hardly stand!" "Wait till we get through with you, see how you'll feel then!" the brothers said, and they went at him with their fists and gave him a sound trouncing.

Some time passed, there was soon to be a holiday, and the old man and old woman sent the fool to town to buy a number of things for the house. Ivan bought all he had been told to, a sack of salt, a table, a set of spoons and one of cups, and lots of other things too, and his wagon was very heavy by the time he had finished loading it. He drove home, but it was slow going, for his old nag was barely able to put one leg in front of the other. "Come to think of it," said the fool to himself, "the table has four legs, too, just like the horse, so why can't it get home by itself!" And he picked up the table and set it down on the road. He drove on, and whether he was near or far from home nobody knows, but by and by the crows began circling over him, cawing loudly as they did so. "They must be hungry to be making such a noise!" thought the fool, and, placing dishes of food on the ground, he called to the crows, inviting them to eat their fill. "Come, my sisters, come, loves, eat and enjoy yourselves!" he cried, and he urged the horse on.

The wagon bumped slowly along. Thinking the fire-scorched tree stumps along the road to be young boys, and hatless, the fool said to himself: "Those lads will freeze, bareheaded as they are!" He stopped the wagon, put the pots he had bought on the stumps and drove on again. He came to a river and began urging the horse to drink, but when it would not, told himself that it did not like the water because it was unsalted. He began salting the water and kept on doing it till no salt was left in the sack, and still the horse refused to drink! "Why don't you drink, you old nag, may the wolves get you!" he cried. "Why, I used up a whole sack of salt just to please you!" He struck the horse on the head with a log and killed it outright. There was nothing left in the cart save the bag in which the spoons were, and this the fool put over his shoulder. He walked along, and with every step he took the spoons went clank-clank as they knocked against each other, and he thought they were saying, "Ivan's a crank!" So he threw them to the ground and began stamping on them, saying as he did so: "Take that, you no-good spoons you! How dare you tease me!"

He came back home and said to his brothers: "I have bought all the things you asked me to buy, brothers!" "Thank you, fool, but where are they?" "Well, the table I set on its legs and it's running after me, the dishes I filled with food and left behind for the crows, the pots I put on the lads' heads so they wouldn't catch cold, the salt I used up for the horse's swill, and the spoons I threw out for teasing me." "All right, then, fool, make haste and bring back all you left on the road."

Back went the fool to the forest, he took the pots from the tree stumps, knocked out their bottoms, strung a dozen of them, big and small, on a stick and brought them home. His brothers gave him a beating, and, leaving him at home to take care of things, rode off to market. The fool sat there and listened for sounds, and he heard the gurgling of the beer fermenting in a barrel. "Stop gurgling, beer, stop teasing me!" said he. But as the beer did not heed him but went on gurgling, he went up to the barrel, pulled out the spigot and let the beer flow over the floor. Then he climbed into a trough, and, using his legs like paddles to push it over the floor, sang songs at the top of his voice.

The brothers came home and when they saw what the fool was doing they put him in a sack, sewed it up and dragged it to the river. They put the sack on the bank and went looking for an ice hole. Now, a landlord happened to be driving past just then in a coach drawn by three chestnuts, and, hearing the pounding of hooves, the fool called out from the sack: "They want to make a governor of me for me to rule people and to judge them, and I know not how to rule or how to judge." "Wait, fool," said the landlord, "you don't, but I do. Come, now, get out of the sack!" he cut the sack open, and when the fool had climbed out of it, crawled into it in his stead. The fool then sewed up the sack again, and, getting into the landlord's coach, drove away. The brothers came back, picked up the sack and let it down into an ice hole, and they heard a bubbling coming from the water. "The fool must be sending up his last bubbles," said they and set out for home. All of a sudden whom should they see driving toward them in a coach drawn by three chestnuts but the fool himself! "Just see what beautiful horses I caught in the river!" he called out boastfully. "And a fourth, a fine bay, is down there still!" The brothers were filled with envy. "Come, fool," said they, "help us get into a sack, sew it up and let it down into the ice hole, and be quick about it! We don't want the bay to get away from us!" Ivan did as they asked and drove home to drink what was left of the beer and to say prayers for his brothers.

The fool had a well, in the well lived a whale, and now I have come to the end of my tale.

Translated by Irina Zheleznova

Good But Bad

A rich man and a peasant were riding along. "Where are you from, my man?" "A good way hence, Sir." "But where?" "From the town of Rostov, Tolstoy is my master." "Is it a big town?" "Haven't measured it." "And is your master strong?" "Haven't wrestled with him." "Why did you leave?" "To purchase something dear: a measure of peas." "That's good!" "No, it isn't." "Why not?" "I was drunk and dropped the peas." "That's good!" "No, it isn't." "Why not?" "I dropped one measure and picked up two." "Well, that's good." "No, it isn't." "Why not?" "There weren't many, but there were lots of pods." "That's good." "No, it's not so good." "Why not?" "The priest's pigs went and trampled all over them." "Oh, that's bad." "No, it isn't." "Why not?" "I killed the pigs and salted two tubs of pork." "That's good." "No, it isn't." "Why not?" "The priest's dogs went and stole the pork." "That's bad." "No, it isn't."

"Why not?" "I killed the dogs and made my wife a fur coat." "That's good." "No, it isn't." "Why not?" "When the silly wench walked past the priest's house, he recognised the fur and took the coat away." "That's bad." "No, it isn't." "Why not?" "I took the priest to court and got his grey mare and brown cow. It was me who won the case!"

Translated by Kathleen Cook

The Miser

There was once a rich merchant called Marko, and no one was more tight-fisted than he. One day he went for a walk and on the way he saw an old man sitting and begging: "Alms for the love of Christ, Christian folk!" Marko the Rich walked past him. At that moment a poor man walking behind him took pity on the beggar and gave him a kopeck. The rich man felt ashamed, so he stopped and said to the poor man: "Hey, fellow. Lend me a kopeck. I want to give the poor soul something, but I've no small change!" The other man gave him a kopeck and asked: "When shall I come to collect my debt?" "Tomorrow!" The next day the poor man went to the rich man to get his kopeck. He went into the big courtyard: "Is Marko the Rich at home?" "He is. What do you want?" asked Marko. "I've come for my kopeck." "Come back later, my man. I really have no small change." The next morning he came and the same thing happened. "I've no small coins. Give me change for a hundred-ruble note, if you like, or come again in a fortnight's time." A fortnight later the poor man again went to the rich man, but Marko the Rich saw him coming and said to his wife: "Quick, wife! I'll take my clothes off and lie down under the icons: you cover me with a sheet, sit down and cry like I was dead. When the man comes for his money, tell him I passed away today."

The wife did as her husband bade her: she sat and wept bitterly. The poor man came into the room. "What do you want?" she asked. "The money I lent

Marko the Rich," replied the poor man. "Well, my good fellow, Marko the Rich is no more. He has just this moment passed away." "God rest his soul! Allow me to be of service to him for my kopeck, mistress; let me wash down his sinful body." So saying he seized a pot of hot water and began to pour it on Marko the Rich. Marko could hardly bear it and twitched his nose and feet. "Twitch as much as you like, but give me back my kopeck!" said the poor man. He washed him down, dressed him fittingly and said: "Go buy a coffin, widow, and we'll carry him to the church: I'll read the psalter over him." So they put Marko the Rich in a coffin and carried him to the church, where the poor man read the Psalter over him.

Night fell dark as pitch. Suddenly a window opened and thieves began to climb into the church. The poor man hid behind the altar. The thieves began dividing up their ill-gotten gains until there was nothing left but a gold sabre, which they were all tugging and would not let go. Then the poor man jumped out and shouted: "Why are you quarreling? Let whoever cuts off the corpse's head have the sabre!" Marko the Rich jumped up in alarm. The thieves took fright, dropped their booty and fled. "Come on, my man," said Marko, "let us divide up the money." So they shared it out equally; both of them had a big pile. "What about the kopeck?" asked the poor man. "You can see for yourself, brother, I've no small change!" And so it was that Marko the Rich never repaid his debt.

Translated by Kathleen Cook

Don't Listen,
If You Don't Like

In our village Luke and Peter had a fight, and the sand clouded up the stream so bright, and the women started brawling with all their might: the lentil soup was wounded, all but dead, the jelly was a-captured, so they said, the radish and the carrot both got ambushed, and the poor old cabbage lost its head. I was lazing in the sun and came too late for the fun.

There were six of us, brothers, all Agafons. Dad's name was Taras, but I don't remember Mum's. Still, what's in a name, eh? Let's call her Malania. I was the youngest of the brothers, but ten times smarter than the others. When everyone to plough went out, we six just waved our arms about. Folk thought we were a-ploughing and waving at the horses. But we were just getting on with our own business.

A buckwheat seed to a whip Dad tied, he swung it hard and threw it wide. 'Twas a fine year for buckwheat, that. The folk came to the field to reap, but we lay in the furrows fast asleep. We lay till noon, then slept all afternoon, but we stacked up the buckwheat, row upon row, from Kazan to Moscow. Then we threshed the whole lot and got a handful of groats.

Next year Dad asks: "Well, my handsome lads so dear, where shall we sow the crop this year?" I was the youngest of the brothers, but ten times smarter than the others. "On the stove," said I. "That is fertile ground. It lies fallow all year round!" Our house was a right biggun. The first row of logs was the floor, the

164

second the ceiling. The windows and doors were bored out with a gimlet. It looked very nice, but there wasn't much room in it.

Dad got up early and worked real hard, stood at the window and stared and stared. The frost crept in and up to the stove: our poor buckwheat really froze. We six brothers racked our brains, what to do to save the grain. I was the youngest of the brothers, but ten times smarter than the others. "We must reap it and stack it away," said I. "But where shall we stack it?" "On the chimney. There's room to spare. " So we stacked it high up there.

At home we had a bald tom-cat: it sniffed the buckwheat and smelt a rat, then gave a pounce and banged its bounce. Down fell the stack into a tub. The six of us racked our brains about how to get the buckwheat out. Then in came our grey mare so nice and ate the buckwheat in a trice; off it trotted, but alas, in the doorway got stuck fast; its belly was swollen from the feast! There it stood and looked about, hind legs inside, front legs out. Then off it galloped like the wind, dragging the house along behind. All this time we laid low, waiting to see what would happen now. When its belly went down again, I grabbed the grey mare by the mane, jumped onto its back and rode off to the inn. I downed some liquor and had a good time; then what did I see but the inn-keeper's gun. "Is it for sale?" asked I. "'Tis indeed," quoth he. So I paid him a pittance and got me a gun.

Off I rode to an oak copse to shoot me some game: there sat a black grouse, and I took aim. But the gun had no flint! It was ten versts or more to the nearest town; by the time I got back the bird would have flown. While I thought thus, my sheepskin coat got caught upon a branch of oak; the grey mare started up with fear and banged my head against a tree—so hard I saw sparks before my eyes. One of the sparks fell on the gun, the gun fired and killed the grouse, the grouse fell on top of a hare, and the hare leapt up and bagged me the catch of my life! So off I set for Saratov with ten cartloads; and sold my catch for five hundred rubles. With the money I got me a wife, the thriftiest woman you've seen in your life: her skirts they do sweep, as she goes down the street; and when little lads meet her, they throw sticks to greet her. No need to buy firewood, so there. I live happily, without a care.

Translated by Kathleen Cook